THE
BLACKBOOK
OF
SECRETS

THE
BLACKBOOK
OF
SECRETS

F.E. HIGGINS

SQUARE
FISH

FEIWEL AND FRIENDS
NEW YORK

SQUARE
FISH

An Imprint of Macmillan

THE BLACK BOOK OF SECRETS. Copyright © 2007 by F. E. Higgins.
All rights reserved. Printed in the United States of America
by R. R. Donnelley & Sons Company, Harrisonburg, Virginia. For information,
address Square Fish, 175 Fifth Avenue, New York, NY 10010.

Square Fish and the Square Fish logo are trademarks of Macmillan and are
used by Feiwel and Friends under license from Macmillan.

ISBN 978-0-312-62905-2
LCCN 2007032559

Originally published in the United Kingdom by Macmillan Children's Books,
a division of Pan Macmillan
First published in the United States by Feiwel and Friends
Square Fish logo designed by Filomena Tuosto
Book design by Susan Walsh
First Square Fish Edition: August 2010
3 5 7 9 10 8 6 4
mackids.com

LEXILE 830L

The text type was set in Monotype Pastonchi, originally designed in 1927 by
Francesco Pastonchi and Eduardo Cotti.

For Beatrix

Non mihi, non tibi, sed nobis

A Note from the Author

I came across Joe Zabbidou's Black Book of Secrets and Ludlow Fitch's memoirs in a rather curious manner. They were tightly rolled up and concealed within the hollow of a wooden leg. How I came to be in possession of the leg is unimportant right now. What matters is the story the documents tell.

Unfortunately neither Joe's Black Book nor Ludlow's memoirs survived the centuries intact, and when I unrolled them, it was obvious that they had suffered damage. Not only were the pages brittle and water-stained, but much of what I had was also illegible. The fragments and extracts are reproduced here exactly as they were written. I corrected Ludlow's spelling—it really was quite dreadful—but I did no more than that. As for the parts that are

missing, what else could I do but draw upon my imagination to fill the gaps? I pieced the story together in the way I thought best. I like to think I stayed as close to the truth as I could with the few facts I had. I do not claim to be the author of this story, merely the person who has tried to reveal it to the world.

—*F. E. Higgins*
England

THE
BLACKBOOK
OF
SECRETS

CHAPTER ONE

FRAGMENT FROM
THE MEMOIRS OF LUDLOW FITCH

When I opened my eyes I knew that nothing in my miserable life prior to that moment could possibly be as bad as what was about to happen. I was lying on the cold earthen floor of a basement room lit by a single candle, no more than an hour's burning left. Instruments of a medical nature hung from hooks in the beams. Dark stains on the floor suggested blood. But it was the chair against the opposite wall that fully confirmed my suspicions. Thick leather straps attached to the arms and the legs were there for one purpose only: to hold down an unwilling patient. Ma and Pa were standing over me.

"'E's awake," crowed Ma excitedly.

Pa dragged me to my feet. He had me in an iron grip, my arm wrenched up behind my back. Ma held me by the hair. I looked from one to the other. Their grinning faces were only inches away from mine. I knew I should not look to them to save me.

Another man, concealed until now in the shadows, stepped forward and took me by the chin. He forced open my mouth and ran a blackened, foul-tasting finger around my gums.

"How much?" asked Pa, drooling with anticipation.

"Not bad," said the man. "Thrupence apiece. Maybe twelve in all."

"It's a deal," said Pa. "Who needs teeth anyway?"

"Someone, I hope," replied the man dryly. "I sell 'em for a living."

And they laughed, all three, Ma and Pa and Barton Gumbroot, the notorious tooth surgeon of Old Goat's Alley.

Once the money for my teeth was agreed with Barton, they moved quickly. Together they dragged me over to the surgeon's chair. I kicked and shouted and spat and bit; I wasn't going to make it easy for them. I knew how Barton Gumbroot made his living, preying on the poor, pulling their teeth, paying them pennies and selling them for ten times as much. I was racked with fear. I had no protection. I was going to feel it all. Every single nerve-stabbing twinge.

They came close to succeeding in their evil quest. Ma was struggling with a buckle around my ankle, her hands shaking from the previous day's drinking, while Pa was trying to hold me down. Barton Gumbroot, that loathsome monster, was just hovering with his gleaming tooth-pull, snapping it open and shut, open and shut, tittering and salivating. I believe to this day his greatest pleasure in life was inflicting pain on others. So much so that he couldn't wait any longer,

and before I knew it I could feel the cold metal of his instrument of torture clamped around a front tooth. He braced himself with his leg on my chest and began to pull. I cannot describe to you the pain that shot through my skull, my brain, and every nerve end in my body. It felt as if my whole head were being wrenched off. The tooth moved slightly in my jaw and another white-hot shooting pain exploded behind my eyes. All the while Ma and Pa laughed like maniacs.

Rage swelled in me like a mountainous wave. I heard a roar worthy of a jungle beast and I was taken over by seething fury. With my free leg I kicked Pa hard and sharp in the stomach and he collapsed on the floor. Barton, caught by surprise, let go of the tooth-pull, and I grabbed it and walloped him around the side of the head. I unstrapped my other leg and jumped down. Pa was groaning on the floor, Barton was leaning against the wall holding his head, and Ma cowered in the corner.

"Don't hit me, Ludlow," she begged. "Don't hit me."

I will not deny I was tempted, but this was my one chance to escape. Pa was almost on his feet again. I dropped the tooth-pull and in a matter of seconds I was out of the door, up the steps, and running down the alley. I could hear Ma screaming and Pa shouting and cursing. Every time I looked back all I could see were Pa's snarling face and Barton's hooked tooth-pull glinting in the yellow gaslight.

As I ran I tried to think where to go. They knew so many

of my hiding places. I decided on Mr. Jellico's, but when I reached his shop the place was in darkness and the blind was down. I hammered on the window and shouted his name, but there was no reply. I cursed my bad luck. I knew if Mr. Jellico was gone at this time of night he might not be back for days. But knowing this was little help in my current predicament.

So where to now? The bridge over the River Foedus and the Nimble Finger Inn. Betty Peggotty, the landlady, might help me. I ran out of the alley and onto the street, but they were already waiting for me.

"There 'e is," screeched Ma, and the chase was on again. They surprised me, Pa especially, with their stamina. I had not thought they would last so long. For at least a half-mile they chased me down the uncobbled narrow alleys and the filthy streets, tripping over bodies and avoiding snatching hands, all the way to the river. Every time I looked back they seemed to be closer. I knew what would happen if they caught me again. The ache in my bleeding jaw was all the proof I needed.

By the time I staggered onto the bridge I was barely able to hold myself upright. Halfway across I saw a carriage outside the Nimble Finger. Just as its wheels began to turn, I clambered on the back, hanging on for my life. As the carriage pulled away the last thing I remember is the sight of Ma sinking to her knees. She was screaming at me from the riverbank, and the monster, Barton Gumbroot, was shaking his fist in rage.

My name is Ludlow Fitch. Along with countless others, I had the great misfortune to be born in the City, a stinking place undeserving of a name. And I would have died there if it had not been for Ma and Pa. They saved me, though it was not their intention, when they delivered me, their only son, into the hands of Barton Gumbroot. This act of betrayal was possibly the greatest single piece of luck I ever had. Ma and Pa's diabolic plan brought about the end of one existence and the beginning of another: my life with Joe Zabbidou.

CHAPTER TWO

Fragment from
The Memoirs of Ludlow Fitch

I didn't know at the time, but I had hitched a ride on a carriage that belonged to, and contained, a Mr. Jeremiah Ratchet. We rattled along for hours, he inside snoring like a bellows, so loud I could hear it above the clatter of the wheels over the ruts, while outside I was clinging to the carriage like an organ-grinder's monkey. The weather worsened and it started to snow. The road narrowed and the potholes became larger, deeper, and more frequent. The driver had no thought for passenger comfort. If it wasn't for the fact that my hands were frozen in position I might well have fallen off. Despite this, and my churning innards (I suffer terribly from travel sickness), toward the end of the journey I was dozing. The carriage began to climb a steep hill, and finally we reached the place that was to be my home for the near future, the mountain village of Pagus Parvus.

Under any other circumstances I would not have chosen to come to Pagus Parvus, but at the time of traveling my

destination was out of my hands. At last the carriage stopped outside a large house and the driver climbed down. I heard him rap on the carriage door.

"Mr. Ratchet," he called. "Mr. Ratchet."

But there was no reply, so he went to the house and rang for the maid. A young girl came out looking none too pleased. The driver called her Polly. Together they dragged the man up the steps, accompanied by much snoring (his) and grunting (theirs) and hauled him inside. I took the opportunity to jump down and sneak a look in the cab, wherein I found a leather purse, a fringed printed silk scarf, and a pair of gloves. I wrapped the scarf around my neck and slipped the gloves over my numb fingers. The purse contained only a few pennies but it was a start. I got out and saw the young girl standing in the doorway looking straight at me. There was a slight smile on her face and her eyes held mine for a long second. I heard the driver coming back and knew it was time to go. I could have gone either way, up the slope or down, but for some unknown reason I chose to climb.

The hill was treacherous. As I climbed I heard the church bell strike four. Although it was no longer snowing, the wind was sharp as a knife and I knew I needed shelter. Despite the hour, and the lack of streetlights, I could see well enough where I was going. It was not the moon that lit my way, for she was only a sliver, but all the lights ablaze behind the windows. It seemed that I was not the only one still awake in this village.

I stopped at an empty building at the top of the hill. It stood alone in the shadow of the church, desolate and separated from the other houses and shops by an alley. I was looking for a way in when I heard approaching footsteps in the snow. I ducked into the alley and waited. A man, hunched over, came carefully down the hill. He was carrying a large wooden spade over his shoulder and he was mumbling to himself. He passed right by me, looking neither to his left nor his right, and crossed over the road.

As he melted into the night another figure appeared. To this day I remember the man emerging from the gloom as if by magic. I watched him climbing steadily toward me. He took long strides and covered the distance quickly. He had a limp, his right step was heavier than his left, and one footprint was deeper than the other.

I believe I was the first person to see Joe Zabbidou and I know I was the last. Was it just coincidence that had us both arrive here together? I suspect other powers were at work. Unlike me, he wasn't fleeing. He had a purpose, but he kept it well hidden.

CHAPTER THREE

Arrival

It was not easy to describe Joe Zabbidou accurately. His age was impossible to determine. He was neither stout nor thin, but perhaps narrow. And he was tall, which was a distinct disadvantage in Pagus Parvus. The village dated from times when people were at least six inches shorter and all dwellings were built accordingly. In fact, the place had been constructed during the years of the "Great Wood Shortage." The king at the time issued a decree that every effort must be made to save wood, with the result that doors and windows were made smaller and narrower than was usual and ceilings were particularly low.

Joe was suitably dressed for the weather, though unheedful of the current fashion for the high-collared coat. Instead he wore a cloak of muted green, fastened with silver toggles, that fell to his ankles. The cloak itself was of the finest Jocastar wool. The Jocastar—an animal akin to a sheep but with longer, more delicate legs and finer features—lived high up

in the mountains of the northern hemisphere. Once a year, September time, it molted, and only the most agile climbers dared venture up into the thin air to collect its wool. The cloak was lined with the softest fur in existence, chinchilla.

On his feet Joe wore a pair of black leather boots, highly polished, upon which sat the beautifully pressed cuffs of his mauve trousers. Around his neck was wrapped a silk scarf, and a fur hat shaped like a cooking pot was pulled down tightly over his ears. It could not fully contain his hair, and more than a few silver strands curled out from underneath.

With every step Joe took, a set of keys hooked to his belt jingled tunefully against his thigh. In his right hand he carried a rather battered leather satchel straining at the seams, and in his left a damp drawstring bag from which there emanated an intermittent croaking.

Quickly, silently, Joe climbed the steep high street until he reached the last building on the left. It was an empty shop. Beyond it was a walled graveyard, the village boundary, within which stood the church. Then the road stretched away into a gray nothingness. Snow had drifted into the shop doorway and gathered in the corners of the flyblown windows. The paintwork was peeling and an old sign in the shape of a hat creaked above the door in the biting wind. Joe took a moment to survey the street down to the bottom of the hill. It was the early hours of the morning, but yellow oil lamps and candles glowed behind many a curtain and shutter, and more than once he saw the silhouette of a person

cross back and forth in front of a window. A smile broke across his face.

"This is the place," he said and let himself in.

The shop itself was quite tiny. The distance between the display window and the counter was no more than three paces. Joe went behind the counter and opened the solid door that led into a back room. A tiny window on the far wall allowed the dusty moon-glow to lighten the gloom. The furniture was sparse and worn: two ladderback chairs and a table, a small stove, and a narrow bed pushed up against the wall. In contrast the fireplace was huge. At least six feet across and nearly three deep, it took up almost the whole of one wall. On either side of the hearth sat a faded upholstered armchair. It was not much, but it would do.

In the depths of the night, Joe busied himself settling in. He turned up the wick and lit the lamp on the table. He unwound his scarf, took off his hat and unfastened his cloak, and put them on the bed. Then he opened his satchel, and as a silent observer peered through the window, Joe emptied it out onto the table. The onlooker never moved, though his already huge dark eyes widened impossibly as Joe pulled out clothes, shoes, a collection of trinkets and baubles, some rather fine jewelry, two loaves, a bottle of stout, another bottle (dark-glassed and unlabeled), four timepieces (with gold chains), a brass hurricane lamp, a rectangular glass tank with a vented lid, a large black book, a quill and bottle of ink, and a polished mahogany wooden leg. The satchel was deceptively spacious.

Deftly Joe fixed the tank together, then took his drawstring bag and loosened the tie. He set it down gently on the table and a second later a frog, a rather spectacular specimen of mixed hue and intelligent expression, emerged daintily from its folds. Very carefully Joe picked it up and placed it inside the tank, whereupon the creature blinked lazily and munched thoughtfully on some dried insects.

As Joe dropped another bug into the tank he stiffened almost imperceptibly. Without a backward glance he left the room, the eyes at the window still following him curiously. But they didn't see him slip out into the street. No human ear heard him tiptoe around the back of the shop, where he pounced upon the figure at the window and held him up to the light by the scruff of his scrawny neck.

"Why are you spying on me?" asked Joe in the sort of voice that demanded an answer without delay.

Joe had the boy in such a grip that he was half choking on his collar and his feet were barely touching the ground. He tried to speak, but fear and shock had rendered him unable. He could only open and close his mouth like a fish out of water. Joe gave him a shake and repeated the question, though less harshly this time. When he still received no answer he let the young lad fall to the snow in a crumpled, pathetic heap.

"Hmm." Joe took a long, hard look at the boy. He truly was a pale and sorry figure, undersized, undernourished, and shivering so hard you could almost hear his bones rattle. His

eyes were striking, though, dark green with flecks of yellow, and set in a ring of shadow. His skin matched the snow in tone and temperature. Joe sighed and pulled him to his feet.

"And you are?" he asked.

"Fitch," said the boy. "Ludlow Fitch."

CHAPTER FOUR

Poetry and Pawnbrokers

Ludlow sat at the table shivering in silence while Joe tended the fire. A blackened kettle hung over the flame and every so often Joe stirred its contents.

"Would you like some soup?"

Ludlow nodded and Joe ladled the thick mixture into two bowls and set them down. The boy gulped his noisily in spilling, overfull spoonfuls.

"Where have you come from?"

Ludlow wiped soup from his chin and managed to whisper. "From the City."

"I see. And do you wish to go back?"

He shook his head violently.

"I cannot blame you. In my experience the City is a rotten, diseased place full of the very worst of humanity. The lowest of the low."

Ludlow nodded again and drank at the same time, with the result that the soup dripped onto his gray shirt collar.

Without hesitation, he put the stained cloth in his mouth and sucked out the juices. Joe watched unsmiling, but with amusement in his eyes.

"And what did you do in the City?"

Ludlow put down the bowl. The warming soup had brought life back to his frozen limbs. "All sorts, really," he said evasively, but then, under Joe's intense gaze, he continued, "though mainly I picked pockets."

"Your honesty is refreshing, Ludlow, but I doubt there'd be much of that sort of work here," said Joe dryly. "This is a small village. There's little to take."

"I can always find something," said Ludlow proudly.

"I believe you could." Joe laughed, looking at the boy thoughtfully. "Tell me, have you any other talents?"

"I run fast and curl up so tight I can hide in the smallest places."

Whether this impressed Joe or not, it was difficult to tell. "Useful, I'm sure," he said, "but what of schooling? Can you write and read?"

"Of course I can," said Ludlow as if Joe was a fool to suggest otherwise.

If Joe was surprised he did not show it. "Then let me see your skill." He rummaged through the pile on the table, then handed Ludlow a quill, a pot of ink, and a piece of paper.

Ludlow thought for a moment, then wrote slowly in his plain, spidery hand, the tip of his tongue sticking out of the corner of his mouth:

> *A Pome*
>
> *The rabit dose be a gentel creture*
> *Its furr is soft, its tale is wite*
> *Under the sun a gras eater*
> *In a burro it doth sleep the nighte.*

Joe stroked his chin to conceal his smile. "Who was it taught you to spell? Your parents?"

Ludlow snorted at the very suggestion. "My parents care not for the written word, nor for me. I was taught by Mr. Lembart Jellico, a pawnbroker in the City."

"Lembart Jellico?" repeated Joe. "How very interesting."

"Do you know him?" asked Ludlow, but Joe was busy looking for another sheet of paper.

"Write this," he said and dictated a couple of sentences, which Ludlow wrote carefully before handing back the paper to be examined.

"Two *b*'s in Zabbidou," said Joe, "but you weren't to know that."

He stood back and took a long, hard look at the boy. He resembled so many City boys, dirty and skinny. He certainly smelled like one. His clothes were barely functional (apart from the scarf and gloves, which were of a much higher quality), and he had a distrustful face that gave away the wretchedness of his past existence. He was bruised and his mouth was very swollen, but there was a spark of intelligence—and something else—in those dark eyes.

"I have a job for you if you want it."

Ludlow's eyes narrowed. "Does it pay?"

Joe yawned. "Let's discuss that tomorrow. Now it is time to sleep."

He threw Ludlow his cloak and the boy curled up in the space beside the fire. He had never felt such soft fur before, and it wrapped itself around his legs almost of its own accord. Ludlow watched through half-closed eyes as Joe stretched out on the bed opposite, his legs not quite fully extended, and began to snore. When he was certain that Joe was asleep, Ludlow pulled out the purse he had stolen from the carriage and hid it behind a loose brick in the wall. Then he took the paper and read it once again.

My name is Joe Zabidou. I am the Secret Pawnbroker.

A secret pawnbroker? thought Ludlow. *What sort of job is that?* But he did not ponder the question for very long before drifting off into a sleep full of wild dreams that made his heart race.

CHAPTER FIVE

Fragment from
The Memoirs of Ludlow Fitch

I hadn't meant to tell Joe I was a pickpocket and I don't know why I told him the truth. As for pawnbrokers, naturally I knew what they were. I'd been in and out of their shops enough times when I lived in the City. Whatever Ma and Pa managed to steal and had no use for, they pawned. Or they sent me to do it. There were plenty of pawnshops, practically one on every corner, and they were open all hours. They were busiest after the weekend, when everyone had spent their wages on drink or lost them at the card table. By midmorning on Mondays a pawnshop window was quite a sight, believe me. People brought in every sort of thing: shirts, old shoes, pipes, crockery, anything that might fetch even a ha'penny.

The pawnbroker, however, wouldn't take just anything. And the money he paid wasn't good at all, but when people grumbled that he was cheating he would say, "I'm not a charity. Take it or leave it."

And usually they took what he offered because they had

no choice. Of course, you could always buy back what you pledged, but you had to pay more. That's how a pawnbroker made his money, getting rich from the poor.

But Lembart Jellico wasn't like the others. For a start, he was hidden away down a narrow lane off Pledge Street. You would only know he was there if you knew he was there, if you see what I mean. I found him because I was looking for somewhere to hide from Ma and Pa. The entrance to the lane was so narrow I had to go in sideways. When I looked up I could see only a thin sliver of the smoky city sky. Mr. Jellico's shop was at the end of the lane, and at first I thought it was shut, but when I pressed my nose against the door it swung inward. The pawnbroker was standing behind the counter, but he didn't see me. He looked as if he was in a daydream.

I coughed.

"Sorry," said the man, blinking. "How can I help you, young lad?" he asked. Those were the first kind words I had heard all day. I gave him what I had, a ring I had taken from a lady's finger (a particular skill of mine, to mesmerize unfortunate passersby with my sorrowful gaze while relieving them of the burden of their jewels). Mr. Jellico's eyebrows arched when he saw it.

"Your mother's, I suppose?" he said, but he didn't push me for an answer.

Mr. Jellico looked as poor as his customers. He wore clothes that people had never come back to claim (and he couldn't sell). His skin was white, starved of the sun, and had a slight shine to it, like wet pastry. His long fingernails were usually black and his lined face was covered in gray stubble. There was always a drip at the end of his nose and occasionally he wiped it away with a red handkerchief that he kept in his waistcoat pocket. That day he gave me a shilling for the ring, so I came back the next day with more spoils and received another. After that I returned as often as I could.

I don't know if Mr. Jellico made any money. His shop was rarely busy, the window was dirty, and there was never much on display. Once I saw a loaf of bread on the shelf.

"Young lass," said Mr. Jellico when I asked him about it. "She swapped the bread for a pot so she could boil a ham. She'll be back tomorrow with the pot and she'll take the bread, a little harder maybe, but it will soften in water."

Such were the strange arrangements between pawnbroker and customer!

I don't know why Mr. Jellico showed me such kindness, why he chose to feel sorry for me over the hundreds of other lads roaming the perilous streets. Whatever the reason, I wasn't complaining. I told him what Ma and Pa were like, how they treated me, how little they cared for me. Many times when it was too cold to stay out, and I was too afraid to return home, he let me warm myself by his fire and gave me tea and bread. He taught me the alphabet and numbers and let me practice writing on the back of old pawn tickets. He showed me books and made me copy out page after page until he was satisfied with my handwriting. It has been remarked that my style is a little formal. I blame this on the texts from which I learned. Their authors were of a serious nature, writing of wars and history and great thinkers. There was little room for humor.

In return for this learning I carried out certain chores for Mr. Jellico. At first I wrote out the price tags for the window, but as my writing improved he let me log the pledges and monies in his record book. Occasionally the door would open and we would have a customer. Mr. Jellico enjoyed talking and would detain them in conversation for quite some time before taking their pledge and paying them.

I spent many hours in the back of the shop engaged in such tasks, and Ma and Pa never knew. I saw no reason to tell them about Mr. Jellico; they would only have demanded that I steal something from him. I had the opportunity, many times, but although I would not hesitate to cheat my parents out of a few shillings, I could not betray Mr. Jellico.

I would have gone to him every day if I could, but he wasn't always there. The first time I found the shop closed I thought he must have packed up and left. I was surprised that he hadn't said goodbye, even though it was the sort of thing I had come to expect from people. Then a few days later he came back. He didn't say where he had been and I didn't ask. I was just glad to see him.

This went on for almost five months until the night I fled the City. As I lay in the fireplace that first night at Joe Zabbidou's I had only one regret, that I had left without saying goodbye to Lembart Jellico. There was little chance I would see him again.

So when Joe said that he was a pawnbroker I was pleased. He seemed different from Mr. Jellico and I knew that Pagus Parvus was nothing like the City, but I felt safe. I thought I knew what to expect. But of course I didn't know then what a Secret Pawnbroker was.

CHAPTER SIX

A Grand Opening

Pagus Parvus was indeed very different from the City. It was a small village clinging for its life to the side of a steep mountain in a country that has changed its name over and over and in a time that is a distant memory for most. It comprised one cobbled high street lined on either side with a mixture of houses and shops built in the style that was popular around the time of the great fire in the famous city of London. The first and second floors (and in the case of the home of wealthy Jeremiah Ratchet the third and fourth floors) overhung the pavement. In fact, sometimes the upper levels stuck so far out that they restricted the sunlight. The windows themselves were small with leaded panes, and dark timbers ran in parallel lines on the outside walls. The buildings were all at strange and rather worrying angles, each having slid slightly down the hill over the years and sunk a little into the earth. There was no doubt that if just one collapsed it would take all the others with it.

The village was overlooked by the church, an ancient building mostly frequented these days when someone was born or died. Entry into this life and exit from it were deemed noteworthy occasions, but for most villagers the intervening existence did not require regular church attendance. On the whole this suited the Reverend Stirling Oliphaunt very well. He didn't seek out his flock; he preferred them to make their own way.

Besides, the hill really was unusually steep.

Despite this, and the snow, by midmorning the next day a small crowd had already gathered outside Ludlow's new home. Even before the sun had fully risen behind the clouds, a rumor was circulating that the old hat shop had a new occupant. One by one the villagers puffed and panted their way up the hill to see for themselves. The murky windows were now clean and transparent, although the varying thickness of the glass distorted the display somewhat, and the people pressed their faces up against the panes, eager to see what was on show.

"Is it a junk shop?" asked one man. A reasonable question under the circumstances, for the contents of the satchel, excepting the food and drink, had been priced with a tag and placed in the window. The wooden leg was propped in the corner, but there was no indication of its cost.

"It's animals," said another.

Joe's frog was clearly visible, sitting in its tank on the counter. In the daylight it was quite remarkable in appearance: Its glistening skin was a patchwork of vibrant reds,

greens, and yellows. It was most unlike any frog that lived in the soupy ponds of Pagus Parvus. Its feet were not webbed; instead they were more like long-fingered hands with knobbly joints and toes, which would have made swimming quite tricky.

As if on cue, Joe's face appeared in the window. He was holding a sign, which he placed carefully at the bottom of the display. It read:

JOE ZABBIDOU ⬯ PAWNBROKER

The villagers nodded to one another, not necessarily in approval, more as if to say "I told you so," even though they hadn't. Joe then emerged with a ladder that he propped against the wall over the door. He climbed confidently to the top and unhooked the old hat-shaped sign. He fixed to the pole the universal symbol of the pawnbroker: three polished golden orbs stuck together in the shape of a triangle. They swung on their chain in a lazy arc, glinting in the low winter sun.

"Is the frog for sale?" someone asked.

"I'm afraid not," said Joe solemnly. "She is my companion."

This admission amused the crowd greatly and their titters created a cloud of breath around their heads.

" 'Ow much for the leg?" asked another. Joe smiled benevolently, descended the ladder with remarkable speed, and stood before the crowd.

"Aha," he exclaimed. "The leg. Now there's a tale."

"A tail?" queried a youngster known less for his wit than for his inquisitive nature, while beside him his two brothers sniggered.

"A tale indeed," said Joe. "But one for another day." There were sighs of disappointment and Joe cleared his throat and raised his hand.

"Ladies and gentlemen, my name is Joe Zabbidou," he announced, pronouncing the "J" with a sort of shooshing noise so it sounded more like "sh." "And I am here to serve you. I stand under the sign of the three golden orbs because I am a pawnbroker, a respectable profession in existence for centuries, of Italian origin, I believe. I give you my guarantee"—here he placed his right hand on his heart and cast his eyes heavenward—"that I will pay a fair price for your goods and take a fair fee when you choose to redeem them. All items accepted: linen and shoes, jewelry and watches—"

"Wooden legs," shouted out a voice.

Joe disregarded this interruption and continued smoothly.

"You have my word. You will not be cheated by Joe Zabbidou."

For a moment there was silence, and then generous applause. Joe took a bow and smiled at his audience. "Thank you," he said as they came forward to shake his hand. "You're very kind."

Inside Ludlow jerked awake from a dream in which he was being pricked with a thousand tiny needles. He sat up to find that the fire had been revived and one of the logs was spitting, sending burning sparks onto his cheeks. Joe was nowhere to be seen, but there was bread and milk on the table, and a jug of beer, and Ludlow realized that he was very hungry. He drank some frothy milk and ate a thick slice of warm bread. He sat back, satisfied, but not for long. Hearing the commotion outside, he went to the door to have a look.

Joe was still shaking hands with the villagers. When he saw Ludlow he nodded in the direction of the crowd, who were milling around, loath to leave this object of curiosity. Joe's arrival was an exciting event for Pagus Parvians. Few strangers ever came to their village.

And a pity they don't, thought Joe as he scanned the eager faces in front of him. There was that hook nose again and again, those close-set narrow eyes, the crooked smiles, each in a different combination on a different countenance.

This place could do with some new blood, he thought. Then out loud to Ludlow he said, "Quite a welcome, eh, Ludlow?"

He turned back to his audience and continued to greet them while Ludlow wondered idly if any had a pocket worth picking.

CHAPTER SEVEN

The Morning After

Halfway down the street, Jeremiah Ratchet was suffering from his escapades of the night before. He had woken with a pounding headache and a raw stomach.

"Cheap ale," he grumbled. "I don't know why I drink in that foul, stinking City."

But of course he did know. He went there because he didn't trust the tavern owners in Pagus Parvus to serve him a decent quart. The one time he had gone into the Pickled Trout at the bottom of the hill he couldn't quite rid himself of the suspicion that the landlord, Benjamin Tup, had spat in his ale. But the accusation didn't go down very well. Besides, he despised the other drinkers, most of whom were in his debt. Jeremiah was happy to take their money but he preferred not to drink with them. And the feeling was mutual.

So Jeremiah went instead to the City, where he sought entertainment in the Nimble Finger Inn on the bridge over the River Foedus. There he drank wine and beer, smoked fat cigars, and played cards until the early hours with a motley bunch of fellows: thieves and gamblers, resurrectionists, and undoubtedly a murderer or two. Although he would never admit it, he felt quite at home in the Nimble Finger.

Jeremiah groaned again when he remembered he had lost a considerable sum of money at the card table.

There's nothing for it, he thought. *The rents'll have to go up.*

Jeremiah liked simple solutions to problems, and rent increases seemed to solve most of his. He did not care about the trouble this caused his tenants. He turned over in bed, but his attempts to sleep again were thwarted by the foul air that wafted up from under the blankets.

Too many onions, he thought as he flung back the curtain and swung his legs over the side. He squinted in the daylight and only then became aware of the noise out on the street. He stumbled and belched his way over to the window to see crowds of people making their way up the hill.

"Polly!" he shouted. "Polly!"

"Yes, sir," she answered, jumping to her feet, for she was only over by the hearth stoking the fire and thinking about the boy with the green eyes she had seen the night before.

"What's all this noise? A man can't sleep with the racket."

"I believe that the hat shop has been occupied, sir."

"By a hatter?" Jeremiah loved to wear a hat, the higher the better. He felt it was a physical measure of his importance. It also gave him the appearance of being taller, for what he didn't lack in overbearing pomposity he lacked in inches.

"I don't know, sir. There's a rumor it's a pet shop."

"A pet shop!" Jeremiah spluttered. "Who can afford the luxury of pets in this place?"

The thought of a single one of his tenants owning a pet was too much for Jeremiah. Although he loved to indulge himself in all sorts of extravagances, it galled him to think that others might, too. So, in a fit of pique, he dressed and staggered up the hill, red-faced and nauseous, last night's alcohol seeping through his enlarged pores. He shoved his hands deep in his pockets and pulled his collar around his neck. His mood had not improved when Polly reported that she had failed to find his gloves, scarf, and purse.

"Blasted coachman," swore Jeremiah as he trudged through the snow. "Thieving, lying hound. Deserves to be whipped."

Polly waited for her master to go some way up the hill before throwing on her own tatty red cloak and following at a safe distance. Jeremiah arrived at the shop just in time to hear Joe's speech, after which he made his presence known (though his neighbors had already caught his odor and moved away).

CHAPTER EIGHT

FRAGMENT FROM
THE MEMOIRS OF LUDLOW FITCH

I stayed in the doorway while Joe stood on the pavement, and I watched as each person approached him. He took whichever hand they offered and enclosed it in his own. At the same time he leaned forward and said something. Whatever it was, it made the women smile and the men straighten up and inflate their chests. I couldn't resist a grin, though I didn't quite know why.

While Joe was still busy shaking hands, a minor commotion started up at the back of the crowd. I stuck my head out a little farther and saw a bulbous man, his face glistening with sweat, pushing his way to the front. The people parted reluctantly to allow his passage. He stood in the snow in a manner that suggested he was supported solely by his own self-importance. He cocked his large head to one side to squint at the golden orbs with a yellowing eye.

There was something very unpleasant about the man: His

bulk was offensive, his stance was aggressive. I was not inclined to make myself known to him, so I stayed where I was.

I suspect Joe had already noticed him but had chosen to ignore him. Eventually, after the man had positioned himself only a matter of feet away and coughed loudly three times, Joe acknowledged his presence and introduced himself.

"Joe Zabbidou," he said, holding out his hand.

The man stared at Joe as if he were a snail on his shoe.

"Ratchet," he said finally, refusing to shake. "Jeremiah Ratchet. Local businessman. I own most of this village."

When I heard the name my ears pricked up. So this was Jeremiah Ratchet, the man who had inadvertently brought me to Pagus Parvus and at the same time brought about a change in my fortunes. His rather grand statement was greeted with quiet snorts of derision from the crowd, even a hiss, and his wide forehead creased in an angry frown. He put his hands on his hips and sniffed, in the manner of a rooting hog. If I had been in that crowd, I would have pinched his purse before he could blink. He was the sort of man who deserved to have his pocket picked. Then again, I thought, as I tried to conceal a smirk, I already had it.

The two men faced each other, Joe's steady gaze taking Ratchet in. Everything about Jeremiah smelled of money: from his perfumed hair to his dark, woolen, three-quarter-length coat; from his mustard-colored breeches right down to the shiny leather of his riding boots. Unfortunately nothing about him smelled of good taste.

"Listen here, Mr. Cabbagehead, or whatever you call your-self. You'll get no business here. You're not needed. These people own nothing of any worth." Jeremiah laughed meanly and puffed out his chest even more. "I should know; most of them owe me back rent."

"We shall see," said Joe, recoiling slightly. Jeremiah's breath was quite pungent. "I have always found in the past that most people benefit from my help."

"Help?" queried Jeremiah. "I don't think we need your sort of help. I help people 'round here. If they need money they know whom to ask. You'll find I provide for the village. You'll pack your bags soon enough."

He turned sharply, satisfied that Joe had been well and truly put in the picture, and strode away with a sort of wide-legged gait that became more ridiculous as he gathered speed.

"Jeremiah Ratchet," I heard Joe say softly, "I think our paths will cross again."

Somehow Jeremiah's presence had cast a sort of gloom over the crowd, and in twos and threes they set off down the hill, holding on to each other for support. Only one person lin-gered, a young girl. I thought I knew her face but couldn't place it until she was almost right in front of me.

"Hello again," she said softly. It was Polly, Jeremiah's maid.

"Hello," I replied, but though I racked my brain I could

think of nothing more interesting to say, so we just faced each other in silence. She looked cold and tired. Her knuckles were red, she wore no gloves, and her fingertips were blue.

"I'd better be off," she said finally. "Ratchet'd be angry if he knew I was talking to you." That said, she turned around and skipped away. I felt a little sorry for her, with her stick legs and red nose. I couldn't imagine Jeremiah Ratchet was the most favorable of masters.

Joe was leaning casually on the ladder, watching us, but suddenly he looked away. I followed his gaze and saw for a second time the small hunched figure with a shovel on his shoulder. He had been right at the back during the whole show, his craggy face expressionless. Now he was going in the opposite direction to everyone else, toward the church. Joe watched him go through the gates, then beckoned to me.

"Hurry," he said and strode off in the wake of the crooked stranger. I pulled the door closed and a little thrill of excitement made me shiver all over.

CHAPTER NINE

Obadiah Strang

An ancient graveyard surrounded the church, and the slope was such that it was impossible to dig a grave without one side being higher than the other. Fortunately for its occupants, Obadiah Strang, the gravedigger, was very good at his job and took great pains to ensure that the floor of each grave was level, so the poor dead soul in the coffin could achieve peace on his back and not on his side. Whenever there was a funeral the mourners were constantly on the move, shifting from one foot to the other as they tried to stand up straight. Only mountain goats that wandered in from time to time seemed at ease, able as they were to keep their balance at any angle. The graveyard must have seemed like a home away from home. Not only that, the grass was particularly rich.

Joe stepped through the rusting church gates, closely followed by Ludlow, and stopped to listen. The rhythmic sound of shoveling came to him on the wind, and when he looked down the slope between the headstones he saw Obadiah Strang hard at work digging a hole.

Stooped even as a youngster, Obadiah had finally reached the age that his bent back had always suggested. He looked like a man who dug holes for a living, and over the years his hands had fixed themselves into the shape of the handle of his shovel. He had great difficulty picking up small objects but was thankful that his clawed fingers could comfortably hold a bottle of ale.

Obadiah continued with his task for quite some time before he noticed that he had company. He clambered out with the aid of a small ladder and stuck his shovel into the pile of earth with some force. Sweat congealed in his eyebrows and he wiped his forehead with the back of his hand, leaving a dark smear. It was not easy to dig a six-foot-deep hole in the winter.

Joe greeted him with a warm handshake. "I saw you at the shop," he explained.

"Ah," said Obadiah gruffly, "you're the pawnbroker. Well, I'll tell you now, you'll get no business from me. I've little more than the clothes I stand up in."

He looked suspiciously at Ludlow, who was hanging back behind a sinking headstone. He didn't like the look of the boy one bit. He wouldn't trust him as far as he could throw him, and that would be quite some distance, seeing as there wasn't a pick of meat on his scrawny bones. Besides, Obadiah never trusted people who didn't blink, and Ludlow's stare was quite unnerving.

"And who's this?"

"My assistant," said Joe smoothly, pulling him forward.

Ludlow smiled and put out his hand, albeit hesitantly. Obadiah ignored it.

"Assistant? You pay an assistant? You pawnbrokers are all the same. You claim poverty but live otherwise." He picked up his shovel, but Joe took him by the arm.

"Wait."

"What do you want from me?" said Obadiah impatiently. "I'm busy."

Joe stared hard into Obadiah's tired eyes. Obadiah wanted to look away, but for some reason he couldn't. His ears filled with a soft noise, like the sea on a rocky shore, and he felt his knees tremble. His fingertips were starting to tingle. Ludlow watched in surprise as the gruff old man seemed to soften and relax.

"You look like a man with a story to tell," said Joe slowly. "Why not come up to the shop tonight? At midnight. No one need know."

Obadiah struggled to get the words out. "Perhaps I will," he said, "perhaps I won't."

"Until then," replied Joe, as if his invitation had been accepted, and he blinked, breaking the spell, whereupon Obadiah had to steady himself on his shovel.

CHAPTER TEN

Fragment from
The Memoirs of Ludlow Fitch

I didn't really understand what had happened in the graveyard. I knew that some sort of arrangement had been arrived at, but its exact nature escaped me. As we left the church grounds I suddenly had the feeling that we were being watched. Out of the corner of my eye, I saw a figure observing us from behind a tree. From his dress I presumed him to be the local vicar. I nudged Joe. He had seen him, too, and he nodded a greeting, whereupon the reverend became very flustered, turned tail, and fled into the church.

Outside the shop the pavement was empty apart from three young boys who ran away as soon as they saw Joe. He laughed as they skidded down the hill. Once inside we went through to the back and sat by the fire. After a few minutes, when Joe showed no sign of talking to me but all the signs of a man on the verge of a snooze, I asked him about my job.

"Your job?" he replied with a large yawn. "I'll tell you later. For the moment just wake me if we have any customers."

And that was it.

I went into the shop and leaned my elbows on the counter, contemplating my situation. The frog watched me for a minute or two and then turned away. Although I had always earned a living, I had never had a job before. I hadn't exactly been raised on the straight and narrow. Pa and Ma together were as big a pair of crooks as ever breathed the Lord's air. They made their living from thievery and I had little choice but to follow in their footsteps, even before I could walk. I was a small baby, and stayed slight. At the age of eighteen months Pa took to carrying me around in a bread basket on the top of his head. He covered me with a few stale loaves. I still remember the terrible swaying from side to side and the fright that kept me rigid. To this day I cannot travel in any moving vehicle without feeling sick.

When the opportunity presented itself Pa would say out of the corner of his mouth, "Lud, me lad," and that was the sign for me to reach out and pinch the hat, and sometimes the wig, of an innocent passing gentleman. Imagine the poor fellow's surprise as his head was bared, leaving him open not only to embarrassment but also to the ravages of the elements. Of course, by the time he looked for the culprits we had long since disappeared into the crowd.

This caper brought in a pleasing sum, since wigs and hats fetched good prices, but inevitably the time came when I could no longer fit into the bread basket. Ma suggested that I be sold to a chimney sweep. My skinny frame more than suited the narrow, angled chimneys. By then I was beginning

to understand that when my parents looked at me with their glassy eyes, they saw not a son and heir but a convenient source of income to support their gin habit. The life of a chimney sweep was harsh and short, and I was supremely grateful when Pa decided I could earn more for them if I learned to pick pockets. Thus, with the minimum of training (spurred on by his belt), I was sent out onto the streets on the understanding that I was not to return without at least six shillings a day for the tavern.

I had little trouble earning this, and any extra I kept for myself. I seemed to have a natural bent for such work: My fingers were nimble, my tread light, and my expression innocent. Sometimes I was a little careless and my victims would feel my fingers in their pocket, but I had only to hold their gaze for a moment to convince them that it was not I who had filched their purse or wallet. If I looked at Ma that way she used to cuff me around the side of the head and hiss, "Don't look at me with those saucer eyes. It don't work on your old ma."

But, you know, I think it did and that was precisely why she got so angry.

She could cuff me only if she caught me, and most days I avoided her and Pa like the plague. When I had earned enough, usually by noon, and needed to warm up, I went to Mr. Jellico's. I couldn't go home even if I wanted to, for Ma and Pa had rented out the room during the day to night workers on the river.

It wasn't such a bad life, not at first, and I didn't know any

other way. I had heard you were supposed to love your parents, but I don't think that is what I felt for them. Some kind of loyalty perhaps, a blood tie, but not love. But once their desire for gin consumed them, my life became unbearable. It didn't matter how much they had, they wanted more. Eventually, whatever I brought home wasn't enough. I suppose that's when they came up with their fiendish plan. I should have known they were up to something. They had started smiling at me.

I shivered when I recalled the desperate chase of the previous night. I could still feel Pa's hand on my shoulder and Ma's screeching voice rang in my head. And then there was Barton Gumbroot's glinting instrument of torture. I couldn't bear to think of it. How strange that I was so far away from it all now.

Joe was still snoring, so I took the opportunity to examine the goods in the shop window. The jewelry was bright and pretty; the hurricane lamp was polished and looked in working order. The timepieces were wound and ticking. Without a second thought I put two in my pocket, but almost immediately a sharp tap on the window made me jump. Polly was right outside. She waved and I wondered how long she had been there watching me. I went out to see her. The snow was packed down where the crowd had been earlier, and she stood carefully on its icy surface.

"It's quiet today," I said.

"Same as usual," she replied.

It was midmorning and my ears listened out for the clashing cries of street sellers shouting their wares, the traveling musicians with their fiddles, the ballad singers, the clatter of cattle hooves on the cobbles on the way to the slaughterhouse, the hissing of the knife grinder's wheel, the rows and fights that broke out on every street corner. But this was not the City, and Pagus Parvus was almost silent. I heard a laugh or two and the blacksmith's hammer but little else.

"Do you want to come in?"

"Can I see the frog?" she asked.

The frog was watching us when we went in. She really was a marvelous creature, her skin bright and glistening like a damp rock. There was no sound from the back room, so I carefully lifted the lid and reached into the tank. The frog seemed a little agitated as I tried to coax her with a bug, and she retreated to the far corner.

"Are you sure you should?" asked Polly nervously.

"Why shouldn't—"

"Don't touch the frog," barked a voice behind me, and I jumped back immediately. Joe was practically next to me and I hadn't heard a sound. An icy blast came in from the open door before Polly slammed it shut on her way out.

"I only wanted to show—"

Joe came forward and replaced the lid, pushing it down firmly. "You mustn't touch her," he said sternly. "Until you gain her trust she only allows me to handle her. Do you understand?"

I nodded and the awkward silence was broken by the sound of the door again and the hesitant inquiry of our first

customer, an elderly lady wearing a monocle in her left eye. She frowned unevenly to keep it in place.

"Mr. Zabbidou? I have an item to pledge."

Joe smiled broadly.

"A lovely piece," he said. "Look, Ludlow, a chamber pot."

CHAPTER ELEVEN

A Midnight Visitor

"Wake up," hissed Joe, shaking Ludlow's arm. "He's here."

Ludlow sat up slowly and listened as the church bell struck midnight. He shivered. The fire had died down and he could see his breath. Joe put a small log on the glowing embers and lit the lamp. He placed two glasses on the mantelpiece along with a dark brown bottle, and then he went to the table and laid his black book in front of the chair.

"Sit here," said Joe to Ludlow. "Stay very quiet, and when I give you a sign, write down everything you hear in the book. I've marked the page."

Ludlow shook off his doziness and sat at the table. He picked up the book and examined it. It was old, but well kept, thick and just too weighty to hold in one hand. On the leather cover in gold leaf were the words, *Verba Volant Scripta Manent*.

In the bottom right-hand corner were the initials *JZ* in large, decorative gold lettering. A piece of red ribbon marked the new page and a quill lay waiting in the crease. The white pages seemed to glow in the half-light, and Ludlow couldn't help but run his fingers over their smooth surface. He quickly flicked through the preceding pages; they were written with a heavy hand and crackled when he touched them. Ludlow had not been told not to pry, but he had the distinct feeling that Joe would disapprove if he did. Quietly he put the black book back down as he found it, open to the clean page.

Outside the pawnshop Obadiah Strang stood on the pavement wringing his gnarled hands. He wanted to knock but he was afraid. Perhaps the dead didn't scare him, but sometimes the living did. Losing his nerve, he turned around and was about to retreat down the hill when the door opened behind him.

"Obadiah, my dear chap," said Joe warmly, stepping into the street and taking the man by the arm, "I've been expecting you."

Once more, under Joe's penetrating gaze, all resistance deserted Obadiah and he allowed himself to be led into the back room and placed gently on the chair by the fire. Ludlow sat without moving, a little nervous, watching everything closely. Obadiah pushed his knuckles into the soft arm of the chair and Ludlow winced as they cracked loudly.

"Will you have a drink with me?" asked Joe. "Something special?"

Obadiah grunted and Joe poured two drinks from the

bottle, handing one to Obadiah. He took his own and sat down opposite the gravedigger.

"Good health," he toasted.

Obadiah took a tentative sip from his glass, and then another longer one. Spirits were not his usual tipple and he'd never tasted one of this caliber. He savored the sensation of warmth as the alcohol ran down the back of his throat. Feeling his knotted shoulders relaxing, he leaned back into the chair.

"Why am I here?" he asked. This wasn't what he planned to say, but it was what came out.

"Because you need help," replied Joe.

"And you can help me?"

Joe nodded and leaned over. "When I look at you, Obadiah, I see a man who has a secret. A secret that is such a burden it threatens to engulf you. It keeps you awake at night and gnaws at your guts every day." He leaned even closer. "It doesn't have to be like that."

Obadiah's eyes were shining. A small tear squeezed from the corner of one and ran down the lines that scored his cheek.

"What can I do?" he whispered desperately.

Joe's voice was soothing and full of promise. "Pawn your secret and free yourself of its terrible burden."

"Pawn it?" Obadiah was a little bemused from the drink, and from Joe's eyes and his soft voice. His head felt as if it were slowly sinking underwater.

"You mean you will buy my secret? But why?"

"It's my business," said Joe. "I am a pawnbroker."

Obadiah shook his head slowly and his brow creased with confusion. "But if I pawn it, then must I claim it back? If I don't, you will have the right to sell it. And if you sell it, then it is no longer a secret." Obadiah liked to make life easy by thinking in a simple and logical fashion.

"Ah," exclaimed Joe. "I think you will find my terms quite agreeable. If you wish to reclaim your secret, then you pay what you took plus a little extra. If not, then I will keep the secret for you for as long as you want, a lifetime if that is your wish. In fact, if you never reclaim it, I will hold it until you are in the grave and beyond, and then I doubt you would care so much."

"Well, I s'pose that sounds fair, Mr. Zabbidou."

Joe smiled. "Let us get started. I am anxious to set a mind at ease."

He nodded discreetly to Ludlow, who realized this was his cue. With a shaking hand he raised the quill and dipped it in the ink. He held the quill poised over the pristine page.

"And you swear you won't tell?" asked Obadiah, quivering.

Joe shook his head solemnly. "Never," he said. "On my life."

"Then hear this and maybe you can help. God knows, no one else can."

For the next hour the only sound in the room was Obadiah's trembling voice and the soft scratching of a nib on paper.

Ludlow's work had begun.

CHAPTER TWELVE

Extract from
The Black Book of Secrets

The Gravedigger's Confession

My name is Obadiah Strang and I have a terrible secret. It haunts my every waking hour, and at night when I finally manage to sleep it takes over my dreams.

I might only be a humble gravedigger but I am proud of it. I have never cheated anyone: They get six feet, no more, no less. I have always led a simple life. I need very little and I ask for nothing. I was a contented man until some months ago when I fell afoul of my landlord, Jeremiah Ratchet.

It had been a difficult week, short on gravedigging and even shorter on tips. When rent day came around I didn't have it. No doubt you already know of Jeremiah Ratchet. He is a hated man in these parts, and I feared what he would do to me. But he surprised me and suggested that I pay double the next week. Like a fool I accepted his offer. But when rent day came again he claimed that I owed him eighteen shillings, not twelve.

"Six shillings' interest on the loan," he explained with an oily smile.

Of course, I didn't have the extra money, and a week later the debt had increased again. I paid what I could and tried to reason with him, but Jeremiah Ratchet must have a hole where his heart should be. After four weeks I owed so much I could never hope to pay.

That was his intention all along.

"I have a suggestion," he said the next time he came over, "a way for you to work off your debt."

Although I distrusted the man by now, I had no choice but to listen.

"I need you to do a job for me, something eminently suited to your skills. I will provide the tools."

Then he explained to me his despicable plan and I flew into a rage and threw him out. He stood on the path and called back to me. "If you will not do it, then I will evict you. You know where I am if you change your mind. I'll give you a week to think it over."

That night I cursed myself again and again for getting myself into debt to the monster. By the time the sun rose I knew that I had no choice. I sent for Ratchet and he came to the cottage to explain what I had to do. He handed me my only tool: a wooden spade.

"Quieter than a metal one," said Jeremiah. "Anyone in this business knows that."

And what a business, the business of bodysnatching.

That night, some time after one, I went to the churchyard

with a heavy heart. How I hated myself for what I was about to do. I knew the grave in question. Hadn't I dug it myself the previous day and watched the coffin lowered into it that very afternoon? And now here I was digging it up again. With every spadeful of dirt I thought of that scoundrel Ratchet. His wealth was made off the backs of the poor. He must have half the village in his debt.

It was raining now and the moon hid herself behind the clouds, ashamed to witness what I was doing. The wind whipped around my head. Water streamed off my hat. The cold froze my hands. The dark clay was sticky with water. It took a supreme effort to raise the shovel; it released only with a loud sucking noise as if the earth herself had come alive and was trying to pull it, and me with it, into the bowels of hell below.

As the earth piled up on the side my sweat mingled with the driving rain. In my chest my heart pounded like a blacksmith's hammer. At last I hit wood. I dropped to my knees and scraped the coffin clean with my hands. The lid was held down by a single nail at each corner. I forced the edge of the spade underneath and began to lever it up. The wood splintered and cracked and split. "Sweet Lord, forgive me," I muttered and crossed myself as a bolt of lightning ripped the sky apart. In its fiery light I gazed down on the poor soul within.

He wasn't a rich man, I could tell from the quality of the finish on the box and the cheap fittings, but who was in these parts? Rich or poor, like us all, he ended up in the dirt. He was young, though, and his handsome face was un-

marked by the accident that had killed him—he had fallen under the wheels of a cart. His pale hands were laid across his chest and his ashen face was peaceful. His earthly worries were over. Mine had just begun.

I hesitated only a second, then took the poor chap by the shoulders and dragged him out of the coffin and up onto the side of the grave. I looked up at the heavens and I swore that this was the first and last time I would do this. I thought that, the soul gone, a body would be lighter, relieved of the burden of life, but I felt as if I were lifting a dead horse. I dragged him across the grass between the headstones to the church gates, where Jeremiah had said there would be someone waiting.

I saw them. Two men dressed in black, their faces and heads hidden beneath hoods. Without a word they took the body and threw it onto the back of their cart between barrels of ale. They covered it with straw and then took off.

I waited until I could no longer hear the horses' hooves before returning to fill in the grave. I worked like a man possessed, shoveling with the energy of a demon, and when it was finally done I went home.

I woke the next day convinced I had dreamed it all, but there by the fireplace was the wooden shovel. I could hardly bear to look upon myself in the mirror. Whatever my reason for doing it, I was still no better than a common body-snatcher. Resurrectionists, they liked to call themselves, but to give a person a fancy name don't change his nature. Doubtless the corpse was now far away, likely as not in the City, under the knife of a surgeon in the anatomy school

and all in the interest of science. At least that's what the doctors said. They paid good money for bodies, and Jeremiah was lining his pockets with it, but never had I thought I would be involved in such a grisly, sinful business.

Jeremiah came knocking that night.

"My men say you did a good job."

It was not a compliment I wished to accept.

"And where are the valuables?" he asked me.

"Valuables? What are you talking about? Isn't it enough that I unburied a body for you? Now you want more?"

He shrugged. "I have it on good authority that that young man was buried with a silver timepiece and a gold ring. Belonged to his father. Strange custom, to bury what could be sold for cash."

I could hardly believe what I was hearing. Ratchet wanted me to be a thief for him as well as a bodysnatcher.

"I did what you asked," I said. "The debt is paid."

He shook his head.

"I think not, Mr. Strang. After all, you owe quite a considerable sum and you haven't collected the valuables. Next time you will have to be more careful."

"Next time?"

I didn't dare to argue anymore, for then I saw what a fix I was in. The penalty for grave robbing was prison at the very least, but only if you were lucky enough to survive the lynching by the dead man's relatives.

That was over six months ago, and Jeremiah has called on me again and again to do his dirty work. I don't like to think

how many bodies I have unearthed. All I know is if I am caught, Jeremiah will not be the one to suffer.

That man enjoys the fruits of my wickedness and I can do nothing about it. I lie awake until the small hours, tortured by my actions. I am betraying the trust of the villagers, a trust I have built up all my life. If they knew they would string me up as soon as they got hold of me.

Jeremiah Ratchet. How I detest that man. If I thought I could get away with it, I'd take a swing at his big, fat head with my shovel. ✳

Ludlow hesitated at that last sentence, but he had been instructed to write everything he heard, so he did. He stole a look at Obadiah, who was as ashen-faced as the very corpses he unearthed. Then he put down his quill, laid a sheet of blotting paper between the pages, and closed the book. Obadiah sat back in the chair, exhausted, and covered his face with his hands.

"You've got to help me, Mr. Zabbidou. I'm a broken man, unworthy of life."

Joe laid his hand firmly on Obadiah's knee.

"Rid yourself of those murderous thoughts," he said. "They will only eat at your soul. There is a natural justice in this world. Perhaps it is not as swift as we should like, but believe me, Jeremiah Ratchet will feel its force. Now, go home and you will sleep, and you will not dream."

Obadiah sighed deeply.

"You know, Mr. Zabbidou, I believe you might be right."
He stood up to go, but Joe held him back.

"Your payment, as agreed." Joe handed him a leather bag
of coins and Obadiah's eyes widened when he felt its weight.

"I'm most grateful to you, Mr. Zabbidou," said Obadiah.
"I can make good use of this."

"And so you should," replied Joe, shaking his hand
warmly. "So you should."

"And what of Jeremiah?" he ventured nervously.

Joe merely blinked once slowly. "Be patient, Mr. Strang.
Be patient."

CHAPTER THIRTEEN

FRAGMENT FROM
THE MEMOIRS OF LUDLOW FITCH

Thus ended my first long day with Joe Zabbidou. It was after two when Obadiah left, and Joe stood at the door and watched him go down the hill and into his cottage. He waited until the lights were extinguished and the place was in complete darkness before coming back in and locking up. I stayed at the table staring blankly at the closed book, my mind spinning at what I had just heard. Now I understood. *It's a book of secrets*, I thought, *and Joe is the Secret Pawnbroker.*

It was difficult to believe that Joe had allowed me to touch such a book, let alone write in it. How I desired to throw it open and read it from cover to cover! What other tales of desperation and despair would I find in there?

I could hear Joe moving around in the shop and talking to the frog. Quickly I opened the book, flicking from page to page, and I read the opening lines of one confession after another:

My name is Eleanor Hardy and I cannot live with my lies any longer . . .

My name is George Catchpole and I have a most shameful secret . . .

My name is Oscar Carpue. In a fit of mindless rage, gripped by madness, I . . .

That was all I managed to read before Joe came whistling back into the room. I snapped the book shut and jumped awkwardly to my feet, knocking over the chair.

"Let us see how you have done," he said, ignoring my confusion and taking the book from the table. I watched nervously as he examined what I had written.

"Excellent work, boy," he said, placing the red ribbon on the next clean page and closing the book. "I doubt I could have done better myself."

A sudden burning flushed my cheeks. I was not used to praise. To cover my embarrassment I pointed to the golden words on the cover.

"What language is this?"

Joe's face lit up. "Ah, Latin," he said. "The language of precision. What is spoken flies, what is written never dies. Remember those words, Ludlow. People believe what they read, whatever the truth of it."

Joe held up the book and spoke quietly. "The stories we

have in here are very precious to their owners and, as a result, of monetary value to others. They have confided in me, confessing their deepest secrets, and it is my duty to protect them. Wherever I go, there is a criminal element, loyal to no one, who would pay well for this and use it for financial gain or worse. But these confessions have been trusted to us, Ludlow, and we must not speak of them outside this room."

Joe did not seem to be including me among those criminals. But just then my hand felt something cold in my pocket and my heart skipped a beat. The timepieces. I still had them. He must not have noticed they had gone. I resolved to return them as soon as possible.

I nodded solemnly. "I can keep a secret," I said.

"I believe you think you can, Ludlow. But I also know what it is to be human. Temptation is a curse to all men."

"I can do it," I said firmly. "Just give me the chance."

For a moment I thought he might say no, but he laughed and said, "What is life if you don't take a chance now and again? I knew a fellow once who only made decisions on the toss of a coin. Should he get up or stay in bed? He tossed a coin. Should he eat or should he not? He tossed a coin. He lived thus for nearly two years until he was struck down by illness. So he tossed a coin to decide whether or not to send for the physician and the coin said yes."

"And he was cured?"

"Well, unfortunately for him, the physician was not the best. His diagnosis was somewhat awry and the medicine he gave was rather too strong, so the poor chap died the next day."

I didn't understand what Joe was trying to tell me.

"You see, Ludlow," he explained, "life is a gamble whatever way you play it. Now, where were we?" He patted the Black Book of Secrets and his tone became more serious. "Of course, if you are to work for me, there are a few things you need to know. First, we always start on a clean page. I make it a rule to go forward, never to go back." He smiled knowingly and stared into my eyes. He knew I had looked in the book.

"And second, when we are finished we must keep it somewhere safe from prying eyes."

I watched as he put the book in no more safe a place than under his mattress. Was this some sort of test? Was he tempting me to steal it?

As I continued to stare he asked me a curious question.

"Do you believe in luck, Ludlow?"

I had thought about this more than once in my life. "I believe some people are luckier than others. Such as those who are not born in the City."

Joe laughed. "Ah yes," he said, "a most unfortunate birthplace. Most born there die there. But you have managed to leave."

"Then I must be lucky."

He shrugged. "Perhaps it is not just luck. Maybe it was Destiny herself brought you here to me."

"Destiny? More like my own two feet!" Then I asked him, "Which do you believe in, luck or Destiny?"

Joe considered for a moment before replying, "We make our own luck, Ludlow, by our actions and our state of mind.

As such you control your own fate. Only one thing is certain: None of us can escape the grave."

Then he surprised me further by handing me a shilling. Although it was unexpected, I took it.

"For a job well done. Add it to the other coins in your purse," he said and winked.

We went to bed soon after that. When I heard Joe's snoring I felt in the crevice behind the brick for my purse and dropped in the shilling. Then I settled down again, wrapped up in the cloak. Sleep evaded me, for my mind was restless. I turned over and thought of Obadiah and Jeremiah Ratchet. Poor Obadiah, he was right to be disgusted at himself; grave robbers and bodysnatchers were considered below contempt. What a cruel irony, for a gravedigger to have to unbury the dead. As I pitied the gravedigger, my contempt grew for Ratchet. He might have brought me to the village, but that was more luck than design.

An hour passed and still I was awake. My mind was thick with confusion. I knew that had Ma and Pa been here they would not have thought twice about hitting Joe over the head and taking the Black Book of Secrets. As for the bottle on the mantel, that would have been downed long ago.

They would have expected no less of me. My instincts—to lie, to steal, to cheat—were bred into me practically from birth. But here, in Pagus Parvus with Joe, they seemed wrong.

I lay in an agony of indecision. My conscience tried to stop me but, I am ashamed to admit, despite Joe's kindness to me and his warning, I gave in. How could I be expected not to do what had come naturally to me my whole life?

Carefully I eased the book out from under his mattress and tucked it in the crook of my arm. I wrapped the cloak around me and crept through to the shop. The frog watched me with accusing eyes and I could hear Joe's deep and noisy breathing. I was surprised to find that the door to the street was unlocked. I pulled it open and stepped outside. It had all been so easy. Not a floorboard had squeaked, not a hinge had creaked. Snow was falling lightly and a glow fell on the street from the lights in the windows. Like last night, most of Pagus Parvus was still awake. If I went now I could go down that hill and never be seen again.

Suddenly I felt the timepieces jarring against my leg and I stopped. I laughed quietly at my own stupidity. What was I thinking? It was the middle of the night, the middle of winter. Behind me was a warm bed and food and someone who seemed to care for me; ahead of me was nothing but white snow and bitter cold.

I hurried inside and placed the timepieces back in the window. With a shaking hand I slipped the Black Book back under the mattress, willing Joe not to wake, and crept over to the

fireplace. As I curled up beside the orange coals I chastised myself.

It was hard to believe that only a day or so ago I had been in the foul City, living the precarious life of a common thief and facing at the hands of my own parents a terrible betrayal. Yet here I was now earning a living, and one more mysterious and exciting than I could ever have imagined. "Ludlow," I said to myself, "you are a fool."

I looked at Joe, fast asleep, and I knew whatever happened tomorrow, and the next day and the next, I never wanted to go back to the City. I might have to live with my past, but here, with Joe, I had a future.

CHAPTER FOURTEEN

Of Frogs and Legs

Ludlow woke the next morning to the smell of warm bread. Joe was standing in front of the fire toasting the heels of a loaf on the end of the poker.

"Just in time," he said, as Ludlow emerged from his nook. "Did you sleep well? I was a little disturbed myself."

"Well enough," mumbled Ludlow, yawning.

Joe dropped the toast onto a plate and sat down at the table. "I forgot to lock the door last night. We could have been murdered in our beds."

Ludlow's cheeks burned as hot as the toast.

Joe continued smoothly. "So, now you've had a chance to think it over, will you stay? It's not a difficult job. You would be a great help to me."

"I should like to stay," said Ludlow. "Very much."

"Then it is settled. Time for breakfast."

In the City, Ludlow's breakfast might have been a moldy crust or hard porridge. In Pagus Parvus, in the back room of the Secret Pawnbroker's, it was a veritable feast. The table was laden with toasted bread, boiled hen's eggs, thick slices of pink ham, a slab of golden butter, and two jugs, one of beer, the other of fresh milk. There was even cutlery, but Ludlow did not let this slow him down and he ate as if he were a condemned man. Joe looked on, marveling at the boy's appetite as Ludlow gulped down a second cup of milk, then eyed the pork pie that sat in the middle of the table.

"The butcher dropped it off this morning," said Joe. "And the baker brought the bread by. Such hospitality."

"Maybe they just want you to buy more of their old junk," muttered Ludlow.

Joe took another large bite of toast and washed it down with a mouthful of beer. He dabbed at his chin with a napkin that lay across his knees. Ludlow had not seen such gentility before, and self-consciously he wiped his mouth with his sleeve. Then for once he waited until he had swallowed before speaking.

"You know," he said, "I feel sorry for Obadiah. I think he is a good man."

"Being good isn't always enough," Joe said.

"I suppose you've heard many stories like his?"

Joe nodded. "And many far worse. But that is little comfort to the poor man. He is right to be scared. If he is caught, then he will certainly be put in prison or hanged from the nearest tree."

"And Jeremiah? What about his part?"

Joe frowned. "He would deny everything. After all, what proof is there that Jeremiah is connected? It is a poor man's word against a rich man's. The verdict is as good as decided already. I fear Jeremiah has such a grip on this village that no one here would dare accuse him, let alone try to convict him."

"Do you think the money is enough?"

"For now," said Joe. "He will be able to pay his rent at least. But I wonder what else Jeremiah has up his sleeve."

"Perhaps we can help him in other ways," said Ludlow.

Joe shook his head. "No, no. I must not interfere in the course of things. Our job is to keep secrets. Once it is in the book, the matter is closed. In fact, we should not even be speaking of it now."

"So is there nothing we can do?"

But Joe was silent.

Business came in fits and starts all day and by closing time Joe's display benefited from the addition of a flower vase in the Grecian style, a pair of leather suspenders with silver clips (one missing), a sturdy pair of scuffed boots (only slightly down at heel), and a set of decorative brass buttons. The chamber pot sat in the corner next to the wooden leg. Toward the end of the afternoon Ludlow was rearranging the buttons in the window when he became aware that he had an audience. Three boys stood outside—the same three who had been in the crowd when Joe had first introduced himself—their heights descending from right to left. They pressed their faces against the window, but they appeared to be shy about coming in. Joe went to the door.

"May I help you young fellows?" he asked and fixed them with his stare.

The youngest proved to be the bravest. "We have nothing to pawn," he said, "but we want to see the frog."

Joe laughed. "But of course, come in," and the three piled in, the youngest pushed to the back now that the invitation was extended.

They were the Sourdough (to rhyme with "enough") brothers, sons of the bakers, Ruby and Elias. They went up to the tank and looked in awe at the colorful creature, which repaid their interest by promptly turning its back to them.

"What's it called?" asked the middle one of the three.

"She," corrected Joe. "Her name is Saluki."

"What does she eat?"

Joe showed them the bags of sticky, writhing worms and shiny-cased bugs that Saluki ate. He allowed them to drop the tasty tidbits into the tank through a hatch in the lid.

"Can I hold her?" This time it was the youngest who spoke.

"May I," corrected Joe. "I know that you *can*. After all, it is not difficult to hold a frog. What you seek is my permission."

"May I?" asked the boy, twitching with frustration.

"No." This request was made again and again on each subsequent visit (the Sourdough brothers came daily), and although Joe agreed that the boys had to be admired for their optimism and persistence, he always refused on the grounds that Saluki was not the sort of frog that liked to be held.

"Would she jump away?"

"She's a tree frog," replied Joe. "More of a climber than a jumper."

"Where did you get her?"

A dreamy look came into Joe's eyes. He hooked his thumbs in his waistcoat pockets and rocked back and forth on his heels.

"She comes from a land on the other side of the world, where the earth curves to the south and there are all sorts of creatures that you couldn't even begin to imagine."

"Did you catch her?"

"She was a gift," he said, "from an old man to a young lad, such as yourselves."

The Sourdoughs tittered.

"Yes, even I was young once," said Joe.

Joe had a tale for the boys almost every day they came up to the shop. He mesmerized them with stories of the far-away lands he had visited, where the mountains spewed fire and molten rock; of the forests where the trees were so tall that it was always cold night on the forest floor and yet their leaves were burned by the sun. He spoke of ships and cities that lay together on the bottom of the ocean, of the frozen wastes where the sun never set. But there was one thing he never told them about, no matter how hard they pleaded, no matter how urgently they begged.

"Tell us about the wooden leg," they implored.

But Joe always shook his head. "Not today," he would say. "Perhaps tomorrow."

CHAPTER FIFTEEN

Wagging Tongues

Polly would have liked to spend as much time in the shop as the Sourdoughs, but while Elias and Ruby were happy for Joe to entertain their boys, Jeremiah was not so lenient and Polly's visits were shorter and less frequent. She and Ludlow still enjoyed their brief chats over the counter, although actually it was more a case of Ludlow listening and Polly talking, for once she got started it was no easy task to stop her. "I don't know what it is about this place," she giggled more than once, "but every time I come in here my tongue just runs away with itself."

Ludlow liked to listen. He was curious about the village and its inhabitants, Jeremiah in particular, and Polly was more than happy to tell him about the goings-on in the large house down the hill.

She told him of Jeremiah's habits (generally bad) and tempers (the same) and unreasonable demands (many and often). Ludlow soon realized that life had not treated Polly well.

She was bright but suffered the disadvantage of little education. In those days ambition wasn't as free and easy as it is today, and although Polly was far from satisfied with her lot she
was resigned to it. Her parents had died when she was only a
baby; Lily Weaver, the local seamstress, had taken her in. Lily
taught her to sew, and indeed Polly showed some skill, but
Lily quickly realized there wasn't enough work in the village
for the two of them, and soon Polly became nothing more
than an extra mouth to feed. Fortunately, or rather unfortunately for Polly, it was about that time Jeremiah Ratchet
made it known that he was in need of a maid. So Polly had
wrapped up her few belongings in an old spotted linen cloth,
tied it to a stick, and walked across the road to Jeremiah's,
where she had lived and worked for the last six years.

"It's not as bad as you might think," said Polly. "As long as
I do what I'm supposed to then he can't complain over-
much." But Polly always looked tired and hungry and Ludlow almost felt guilty that he worked for Joe, Jeremiah's
complete opposite.

"It was better when Stanton Cleaver was around," Polly
told him one day.

"Stanton Cleaver?" asked Ludlow.

"The butcher's father. When I first came to Jeremiah's, he
and Stanton used to eat together nearly every night of the
week. It gave me some peace."

"What happened to him?" asked Ludlow.

"He had a bad heart, at least that's what Dr. Mouldered

said, and he died very suddenly. They buried him so quickly no one even saw the body. Everyone thought Stanton was a great man, but I'm not so sure. He treated Horatio, his son, really badly. Anyway, after Stanton died Jeremiah didn't have any more friends in the village, so he started gambling in the City. He's still at it, and I never know if he's going to come in late or early, but whatever the time, he's always drunk." She sighed. "I don't understand why you left the City to come to this place, stuck out here in the middle of nowhere. Was it really that bad?"

"It's much worse than I told you," said Ludlow grimly. "You'd hate it, Poll. It's full of all sorts of nastiness."

"Some people say that you left the City because you committed a crime," said Polly. "They think you're on the run."

Ludlow frowned. "Let them think what they want."

"And what about Joe?" she persisted. "Where did he come from?"

Ludlow shrugged. The few times he had asked, Joe had avoided the question very successfully. Ludlow did not actually know very much about his new master. Even in the exotic stories he told to the Sourdough brothers Joe somehow managed to give little away.

"Anyway," said Polly with a grin, "no matter. He's got Jeremiah in a proper lather. You should hear how he curses the pair of you. One day he really will explode!"

Whatever Jeremiah Ratchet thought of Joe and Ludlow, the villagers made good use of the pawnshop. True, they owned little of any great value, but unlike most pawnbrokers, Joe took everything he was offered, even the most ridiculous and worthless items—a moth-eaten, slightly moldy stuffed cat being one such example—and paid good money as he promised. Ludlow could not imagine even Lembart Jellico accepting such a pledge.

As most customers came in wheezing after climbing the hill, Joe instructed that a chair be set by the door, and it was gratefully received. Ludlow watched them from behind the counter, gasping and coughing and complaining. Eventually the noise would subside and they would come over to show whatever sorry item they had brought. Joe would hold it up to the light and turn it this way and that. Sometimes (but very rarely) he would take out his jeweler's glass and examine the object close-up. All the while the customer stood by hardly breathing, fists closed and white-knuckled, hoping that Joe would take the useless object. He did of course, and they were all grateful, immensely so, and thanked Joe profusely. Often that was the end of business and they would back out of the door still saying thank you. But sometimes the person hung on, hopping from one foot to the other, pretending to be interested in Saluki.

Eventually Joe would turn around and ask quite innocently, "Is there anything else?" The hint of a smile danced at the corners of his mouth.

Invariably they would talk about Jeremiah Ratchet.

"You must be a brave fellow, Mr. Zabbidou. There's not many would stand up to Jeremiah."

They were referring to that first day when Joe had dared to disagree with Mr. Ratchet. It had made a great impression upon the villagers.

Joe's response was always the same. "I simply stated the truth."

"He's thrown another family out on the streets, you know," they would continue, undeterred by Joe's apparent indifference. "At least, he had those brutes do it for him. They wear masks over their faces so we don't know who they are. And for the sake of a few pennies' rent, Mr. Zabbidou. It's not right."

If they expected Joe to do something about it, they were disappointed. He merely shook his head sadly.

"A terrible business," he said. "A truly terrible business."

CHAPTER SIXTEEN

FRAGMENT FROM
THE MEMOIRS OF LUDLOW FITCH

The City was gray from dirt and disease; Pagus Parvus existed in a gray light that was cast by clouds that never seemed to go away. I soon learned the weather in the region varied little from what I had experienced the night I arrived. Sitting as it was on the exposed side of a mountain, covered in snow eight months out of twelve and rained on for the other four, Pagus Parvus was not popular with outsiders, and those who lived there left it rarely. Although rumors had reached them of a vehicle that moved by itself, they had not yet seen one of these great iron beasts, and the parallel tracks it rode on were not coming in the direction of Pagus Parvus. If given a choice Pagus Parvians preferred to travel by horse and carriage, but that was a privilege of the few, so mainly they were on foot.

If it had not been for Joe there was little to keep me here, but still I began to think of it as home. My days as a pickpocket were long over and I was glad not to have to

thieve anymore. I continued to wear Jeremiah's gloves and scarf, however. It was worth it to see how he stared whenever we met.

At night, after supper, we would sit by the fire and talk. We discussed many things but seldom reached any conclusions. Joe was a man of few expressions; his face rarely gave anything away, although he became quite animated when we talked about Saluki. That frog was treated like a queen. Joe fed her the finest bugs and snails and worms and the Sourdough boys were up almost every day just to fuss over her.

We also talked about Jeremiah Ratchet. Whenever the shop bell rang I had taken to guessing whether it would be a pledge or merely another complaint about Jeremiah. The blustering buffoon had practically the whole village beholden to him. He seemed to spend his days either threatening to evict his tenants or sending his masked men to do just that. Every time I heard his name I became more and more frustrated that no one in the village seemed willing, or able, to challenge him.

"Why do you think the villagers tell you so much about Jeremiah Ratchet?" I asked Joe.

"Because they are impatient."

It was a typically brief reply. Sometimes conversations with Joe were like riddles.

"Jeremiah," he continued, "is a heavy burden for a small place like this."

"Then why don't they do something? There are enough of them."

Joe shook his head. "Jeremiah is a cunning fellow. Each person is so caught up with his own predicament that he cannot see true strength is in the crowd. To overthrow Jeremiah they must work together, but he has them divided and held hostage to their fears. They believe he has informers in the village."

"Surely the villagers wouldn't betray each other?"

"No doubt they are forced to," said Joe. "And because they cannot trust each other they are unwilling to plot against Jeremiah in case he finds out. They talk to me because I am a stranger and Jeremiah has no hold over me. In their desperation they think I might save them from that scoundrel."

"And will you?" I asked. Silently I willed Joe to take him on.

"However bad the situation, I cannot change the course of things," he replied, and would not be drawn on the subject any further.

I cannot count the number of times Joe said this. It always left me wondering: Was he suggesting that he knew the course of things? And although he maintained that he was unwilling to bring about change, his very presence had already had a noticeable effect on the villagers. After all, he had come to Pagus Parvus a stranger, opened his shop, and in a matter of days he had gained the respect and admiration of all around him. We were all drawn to him, like the moths that fluttered noisily outside the lighted windows at night. Some people make their presence known with loud voices or grand gestures, but Joe didn't have to do that. He was a soft-spoken

man who didn't waste words. But you could just feel when he was near.

As for how Joe made a living, well, that was a complete mystery to me. After all, what sort of business was it to give money away? How else could you explain what he was doing? The window display was growing daily, but although he paid for many items, I rarely saw him sell anything.

And then there was the Black Book of Secrets. Pagus Parvians were quick to take advantage of the service he offered, and at midnight Joe was handing out bags of coins to all and sundry. There were many secrets in Pagus Parvus. During the day the place seemed nothing more than what it was, a small mountain village. It was only in the hours of darkness that it became obvious all was not well. All those wakeful nights I spent looking down the hill, I knew that behind the windows each glowing lamp, each flickering candle, told a tale. Shadows moved across the curtains, silhouettes paced in the dark, pressing their knuckles against their foreheads in frustration and guilt.

Joe listened intently to every tale of woe, and regardless of the confession, he never passed judgment. I know he paid well, but I did not know upon what basis Joe calculated a secret's value. I did ask him once where his money came from and he simply replied, "Inheritance," and made it clear the conversation was over.

Elias Sourdough came up one night from the bakery and admitted that he had been cutting the flour with alum and chalk. That was worth four shillings. When Lily Weaver came

by and said she had been cheating her customers out of cloth by using a short measure, he gave her seven. Even Polly paid us a visit, sneaking out of Ratchet's house late one night to admit to stealing his cutlery. Joe, and I, knew this already. Polly had pawned a knife and fork only two days previously, but it wasn't until she was gone that we noticed Jeremiah's initials on each piece. I had to admire Polly's cheekiness. She knew we couldn't put them in the window (though wouldn't I have loved to have seen Jeremiah's face at the sight of his own cutlery on display). Instead Joe used them for his dinner.

Each night Joe stoked up the fire and set the bottle of liquor and two glasses on the mantel and I took the Black Book from its hiding place and filled the inkwell. Then we sat and waited, he in his chair by the fire and I in mine at the table. There was hardly a night went by without a knock on the door as the church bell struck twelve. I played my part. As the villagers gave their confessions, I sat in the shadows and wrote it all down, word for word.

Sometimes it was hard not to shout out at what I was hearing. Every so often I would sneak a look at Joe sitting by the fire resting his elbows on the arms of the chair, his fingers slightly touching. His face was like a blank page, whatever was said. Very occasionally he would bend back his forefingers for a split second, make circles in the air with the tips and then bring them back together again. But not once did his expression change.

CHAPTER SEVENTEEN

Horatio Cleaver

"He's a murderer," hissed the oldest Sourdough. "He takes his chopper in the middle of the night and goes hunting for fresh meat. Man meat."

"And he puts it in his pies," added the middle brother, while the third, the youngest, began to whimper.

The three boys stood outside the butcher's window watching as he sharpened his knives. They loved the scrape of the blade on metal and to see the sparks that flew around his head.

"If you know this," asked the youngest tremulously, "how come he's not in jail with all the other murderers?"

His brothers poured scorn on this ridiculous suggestion.

"There's no proof, stupid. You can't put a man in prison without proof."

"And the proof is in the pies," said the other. "By the time the murder is discovered, it's too late."

"Yeah, cos they've been eaten!" shrieked the pair in unison.

As for Horatio Cleaver, the subject of this slander, as soon as he saw their wet noses against the window he roared at them and ran to the door and shook his knives violently in their direction.

"Get your filthy noses off my p-p-panes," he shouted.

The trio ran away screaming and laughing, tripping and skidding down the icy hill with their arms flailing.

Ludlow and Joe arrived just in time to see the Sourdough boys disappearing in the distance. Horatio was still standing at the door of his shop, his fists clenched, when he noticed them. They were a strange sight. Joe stood out from the crowd and not only on account of his unusual height. He strode with a confidence, despite his limp, that was both disarming and enviable. Even people who had lived in the village all their lives could not negotiate the steep icy slope with such ease. Ludlow was always a few steps behind, no higher than Joe's elbow, trotting to keep up.

Horatio quickly slipped back inside behind the counter. Joe stood for some moments looking in the window, eyeing the butcher's wares. Today he had for sale a selection of "Prok Peyes," a "Brayse of Fessants," best "Lam Clutets," and "Hole Pukled Chikins." Horatio had not often seen the inside of a schoolhouse.

"I won't be long," said Joe, and he went in, leaving Ludlow outside, where he stood and watched.

As a butcher, Horatio Cleaver was far from the best, but he was the only one the village had so people made do. His father, Stanton Cleaver, had been renowned near and far for his meat-carving skills and was remembered fondly by all his customers. He could butcher a whole cow, head to tail, in under three minutes, a feat he performed annually to wild applause at the county fair. Who could forget the sight of Stanton holding up the Butcher's Cup to deafening cheers, his white apron sodden with blood and his hands stained pink?

Horatio certainly couldn't and, unfortunately, he was never likely to take his father's place on that stand. He was reminded of this fact every day when he heard the disappointed sighs of his customers and the "tut-tuts" as he hacked at their joints and their chops. But they always took the rather roughly hewn cuts of meat he handed them, for if they got more than they asked for, they certainly paid less than it was worth. Horatio had never been good with numbers and the complex relationship between weight and price was one he hadn't quite managed to grasp.

And if it wasn't the customers sending him scornful looks it was Stanton himself, for painted on the wall behind the counter was a life-size portrait of the man complete with a boning knife in his hand and a sneer on his face. Horatio could feel his eyes boring into the back of his head and he grew nervous and stammered—a legacy of his time serving his father. It was only on his p's, however, and most noticeable when he was nervous or his temper was roused.

Stanton was not an easy man to forget. Despite the fact that he had been in the grave nearly five years, he had a long reach. Late at night Horatio would wake, gasping for breath as if the master butcher's hands were around his neck, suffocating him. Horatio had not had a happy apprenticeship, and his father had often been driven to violence by his son's poor butchering skills.

Horatio had started in the shop as soon as he could reach the counter, and over the years the young butcher had begun to take on the appearance of the meat with which he worked all day. He had gradually become more solid in the body, rather like a bull, and his thick, hairless forearms were shaped like two shanks of lamb. His skin was the color of hung meat, a sort of creamy blue, and of similar texture. His face was long and his nostrils flared and his brown eyes surveyed his surroundings with mild interest. The tips of his fingers were thick and blunted; for a man who made his living working with knives he was surprisingly careless.

Horatio wiped his bloodied palms on his graying striped apron and greeted Joe with a pleasant "Good afternoon" and a nervous smile. He nodded in the direction of the fleeing children.

"I should make sausages out of them," he joked, the blades of his knives glittering in the lamplight. Outside Ludlow shuddered at the sight.

Joe laughed politely. "Let me introduce myself," he said. "I am Joe Zabbidou—"

"The p-p-pawnbroker," interrupted Horatio.

Joe responded with a small bow.

"You're up in the old milliner's shop. I hope you do better than Betty P-p-peggotty."

Joe raised his left eyebrow quizzically.

"She made hats," continued Horatio, blowing on his huge red hands. The temperature in the shop was only marginally higher than outside. "Very expensive, mind. P-p-peacock p-p-plumes, ostrich feathers, silk flowers, and all that sort of thing. Not to my taste. Too fancy. Me, I like a p-p-plain hat." He touched his white butcher's cap proudly and left specks of gristle on the brim.

"So I see."

"She couldn't make any money so she went to the City, to run an alehouse, I believe." He secured a piece of pork to the counter with the heel of his hand and hacked at it absentmindedly with a knife.

"Wrong location, see. Too far up that cursed hill. No one goes up that end these days unless they're laid out in a box. Even then they have to be p-p-pulled up. Takes six horses. And the noise of that coffin on the cobbles! Would wake the dead." He stopped, knife in midair, to laugh at his own joke.

"They come up to me," said Joe.

"So I've heard. Well, maybe you'll have more luck than she did."

"Jeremiah Ratchet thinks not."

Horatio spat with contempt into the sawdust.

"Didn't take him long to stick his oar in."

"He said he was a businessman."

"P-p-pah!" exclaimed Horatio. "That slimy toad. I'll wager he's made a deal or two with the devil in his time. He lives off the backs of the p-p-poor. Lending money, then taking all they have when they can't p-p-pay it back. Throwing them out of their homes for the sake of a few days' rent. He'll bleed this village dry. No wonder he got on so well with my father; they were cut from the same cloth."

He brought down his knife with a tremendous crash, sending a huge pork chop spiraling into the air and over the counter. Joe caught it with lightning speed.

He looked straight into the butcher's sad eyes and though Horatio wanted to look away, for some reason he couldn't. His ears filled with a soft noise, like wind through trees, and he felt his legs go weak. His deadened fingertips seemed to have developed pins and needles.

"You sound like a man who needs to get something off his chest," said Joe quietly. "Come up to the shop tonight. Maybe I can help."

"I doubt it," replied Horatio slowly, mesmerized by Joe's gaze.

Joe was insistent. "After midnight, so no one knows."

"Perhaps."

"Excellent," said Joe, smiling broadly and breaking the spell. "Until then."

"What about my p-p-pork chop?"

"I'll have it for my supper," said Joe. "I'll pay you later, when you come up."

The church bell sounded midnight as Horatio pulled his coat closer and raised his fist to the door. The pale half-moon watched quietly as he dithered, in two minds whether to knock. He hadn't meant to come and he didn't really understand why he was here, but as midnight approached his restless feet had taken him out of the door and up the hill. How could this stranger help him? In fact, how did this stranger even know he needed help? He remembered how Joe had looked at him. Had he sucked his thoughts out of his head?

Horatio raised his fist, but before he could strike the wood Joe opened the door.

"Horatio, come in," he said warmly. "We've been expecting you."

He led the silent butcher into the back room, where the fire was blazing. Horatio lowered his sturdy frame into the offered chair and frowned as it creaked alarmingly. Joe handed him a glass of the golden liquid and he took a long draught, then another. His cheeks flushed and his eyes shone.

"A powerful drop," he said and drained his glass.

"I believe you have a secret you'd like to pawn," prompted Joe.

Horatio's eyebrows met in a quizzical frown. "What do you mean?"

"It is what I do," explained Joe. "I buy secrets."

Horatio considered the proposal for a short moment. "Then buy this," he said.

Ludlow was already settled at the table, the Black Book open before him, and Horatio began.

CHAPTER EIGHTEEN

EXTRACT FROM
THE BLACK BOOK OF SECRETS

The Butcher's Confession

My name is Horatio Cleaver and I have a dreadful confession.

Guilt has driven me to the brink of madness. I cannot sleep. Instead I pace the floor until dawn, going over and over in my head what I have done. I desire only one thing: to be freed of my terrible burden.

I know people think I am a fool, both as a man and as a butcher. I lack the talent that my father, Stanton, had and I am the first to admit it. He was a true master of his trade. His skill with a cleaver was unrivaled and he won every butcher's competition in the county for his speed and precision. They called him Lightning Stan. To Pagus Parvians he was the greatest hero since Mick MacMuckle, the one-armed blacksmith who could shoe a horse blindfolded.

To me he was a beast.

When my mother was alive I was spared the worst of his

excesses, but she died, still a young woman, and I was left at his mercy. He was a sly fellow, you see. To the villagers he was a cheerful chap, always ready to flatter the ladies and joke with the gentlemen. But away from the counter, out the back in the cold store, he was a different man. He was a monster. He beat me every day with anything he could get his hands on: pigs' legs, rump steaks, even chickens with their feathers still on. All the time he told me I should be grateful to him for teaching me his trade.

"Nobody else would have you," he said and I began to believe him.

I was so nervous that I made even more mistakes and he became angrier. He laughed at my spelling, yet wouldn't allow me any schooling; he mocked my stammer, knowing that only made it worse. As for my work, I did my best but I'm no carver—I'm all fingers and thumbs, what's left of them. As punishment, or for a joke, he would lock me in the ice store until my hands were so stiff I couldn't bend them around a knife.

My life was miserable. At night I slept on the sawdust behind the counter while he snoozed upstairs in front of a warm fire with a glass of whisky. I wanted to run away, but he had me so scared I couldn't think straight. So I suffered the lashing of tongue and belt, and inside I seethed like a mountain about to explode.

And then there was Jeremiah Ratchet. My father saw in Jeremiah a kindred spirit—namely a glutton with an insa-

tiable appetite for money—and the two would sit by the fire in the room above the shop well into the early hours sipping ale and brandy while I waited on their every whim.

"P-p-pour us another, p-p-please, Horatio," Jeremiah would say mockingly and the two would burst into throaty laughter. Or, "Remind me, Horatio, how much is your lamb?"

"Twelve p-p-pennies a p-p-pound."

One day Jeremiah came in laughing. "I see you have a new product," he said, pointing to a sign in the window, a sign I had written. To my shame it read: "Micemeat Peyes—three pense eech."

"Micemeat pies?" bellowed my father, grabbing a chicken, his face puce with rage.

That night I realized I had nothing left to lose. The time had come to fight back. They say revenge is a dish best eaten cold. I served it up hot and steaming.

The next evening my father sat down as usual to a hearty meal of potatoes and pie, one of my own creations, and Jeremiah joined him as he often did. To see these men at the table was repulsive in the extreme. They ate as if they had only hours to live. Barely was one mouthful masticated before another was crammed in. Gravy dribbled down their chins, piecrust clung to their greasy cheeks, and their napkins were spotted with food.

I watched, fascinated and repelled at the same time, as they tucked in. For they had just eaten a very special pie. Micemeat indeed!

The next morning I woke to the sound of agonized screams from upstairs. I found my father groaning and writhing on the bed. His face was covered in pus-filled boils, sweat ran from his brow, and his breathing was rapid and painful. He was clutching at his stomach and every so often he would let out a screech of pain. I called for Dr. Mouldered, but by the time he arrived it was clear to us all that my father was on the verge of death.

Mouldered seemed perplexed. "Well, although I think it is probably a malfunction of the heart, I am a little puzzled by the boils. How peculiar. Has Mr. Cleaver been bitten by a rat?"

I could feel my own face burning and my heart racing. Whatever his illness, it wasn't from a rat bite, more likely from biting a rat. Possibly the one I had served up to him in the pie the night before. Or maybe it was another of my ingredients. The recipe was simple: If it was dead it went in— hair, fur, paws, claws, and all. There was a minced mouse, two fistfuls of hard-back beetles, plump bluebottles, and juicy purple worms, not forgetting the toad I found on the road squashed by a cartwheel.

I watched my father for a day and a night, and all the time he moaned in agony I berated myself for my stupidity. I had only wanted to punish him. I didn't want him to die.

But die he did.

He exhaled his last breath as I stood over him. And what did I feel? Everything: remorse, guilt, rage—and relief. I closed his eyes, covered him up, and went for Dr. Mouldered.

"Heart attack," he said wearily without even opening his bag and left almost immediately.

Of course, the villagers mourned his passing.

"What shall we do without Stanton?" they cried. "Who shall represent us in the county competition?"

"I could try," I said once and they looked at me as if I were a piece of gristle in a cheap pie.

Well, with my father gone my life should have taken a turn for the better. But I hadn't reckoned on the guilt that would consume me, or on Jeremiah Ratchet.

A few days later he paid me a visit. I hadn't seen him since the night of the fatal meal. He was as white as a leaf starved of the sun and his bloodshot eyes were sunken into his dry flesh.

"I have a bone to pick with you," he said sternly. "Or should I say foot?" He held out his hand and there on his palm was a tiny but unmistakable rat's big toe.

"I found it between my teeth," he said. "After that pie you served us, the one that made me sick as a pig for the last three days. The same pie that killed your father. I see you buried him quick enough."

My heart froze in my chest but I managed to stammer, "Mr. Ratchet, what do you mean? If the p-p-pie killed my father then how come you are still alive and well?"

Ratchet narrowed his eyes. "Obviously I didn't eat the rest of the poisoned rat."

He leaned over the counter so I could smell his sour breath.

"I'll be keeping an eye on you," he said.

And he left, but not before helping himself to a couple of fine steaks and a piece of mutton, although he ignored the pies. And because I didn't stop him Jeremiah knew that he was right.

What a cruel and fickle mistress Fate is: to kill one and yet to leave the other to torture me. Ratchet comes every week and takes what he pleases: a goose or two, a pheasant, a piece of beef. How long will that satisfy him? What will happen to me if he tells? I know what I did was wrong, but must I suffer on its account for the rest of my life? Is there no respite from this agony?

I am not a man without a conscience, I am deeply ashamed of what I have done, but I don't know how much longer I can endure this torture. I have not slept through the night since the day my father was buried. ✳

Ludlow put down his quill, laid a sheet of blotting paper between the pages, and closed the book.

"I can give you respite," said Joe, and he looked into Horatio's troubled eyes. "Your secret is safe in the book now, I swear to you."

Horatio sighed deeply and the lines on his brow slowly disappeared. His eyes brightened and he yawned widely.

"I feel better already." He stood up, but hesitated to take the coins that Joe offered, a substantial amount.

"Mr. Zabbidou, I feel it is I who should be paying you!"

Joe shook his head. "Not at all, Mr. Cleaver. It is a fair exchange."

"Very well," said Horatio and made his way to the door, where he stopped for a moment. "I swore I would never bake a rodent pie again, but I cannot deny there are days when I am tempted. Every time Jeremiah Ratchet comes in, striding about as if he owns the place, flaunting his posh clothes and smelling like a perfumery, wouldn't I like to give him one more special."

"The day will come when you will not have to suffer that man any longer," said Joe. "Ratchet'll get what's coming to him. Just be patient."

Joe took Horatio to the door and Ludlow sat silently at the table. Horatio's story had reminded him of things he wished to forget. Ludlow knew what it was like to have a violent father. What bad luck for Horatio to be born to such a man. But did that mean he had been destined from birth to murder him?

Joe watched as Horatio made his way back to the butcher's. He waited until he saw him go into his shop and the light go out upstairs. He smiled. Horatio was going to sleep tonight. But there were others who wouldn't.

CHAPTER NINETEEN

A Disturbed Night

While Joe was listening to the woes of the villagers, halfway down the hill Jeremiah Ratchet lay wide awake in his bed. Prior to Joe's arrival, it was rare to see a light on after midnight in Jeremiah's house. A man with no conscience often sleeps soundly, and Jeremiah would snore hour after hour (keeping Polly awake up in her attic bedroom), blissfully untroubled by the fact that he was the chief cause of insomnia in Pagus Parvus.

Now Jeremiah spent his nights tossing and turning. He called for Polly at ungodly hours, requesting a warm drink or a book to read or fresh hot embers for his bed warmer. But nothing worked. Sleep would not come.

Jeremiah Ratchet lived right in the middle of the street in a house that was five times the size of those he rented out to his unfortunate tenants. He had spent many years filling it with all sorts of treasures, but in the end the effect was similar to his clothing: loud and difficult to miss, and not a

pleasant sight. The house had seven bedrooms (though he had never entertained an overnight guest), a marvelous dining room served by a large kitchen (most nights he ate alone), and room for five servants in the attic (his innate meanness meant he kept only two: Polly and a boy to look after his horses, but he slept in the hay).

Jeremiah used to take great pleasure from wandering the musty, shadowy corridors with his hands clasped smugly behind his back. He contemplated the portraits on the stairs: seven generations of Ratchets watching him with cold eyes and curled lips. He admired the shine on his silver and reveled in the luxury of his imported rugs—hand-tied by carpet weavers in an African desert. Sometimes when he dug his fingers into the pile he imagined he could feel the grains of sand under his nails. In fact, it wasn't his imagination. Polly's cleaning left much to be desired.

But this was all before Joe Zabbidou arrived.

Joe had rattled Jeremiah from that very first morning. Although he had not gone up to the shop since then, not in daylight at any rate, Ratchet knew what was in the window. Polly had been instructed to pay regular visits—although not to enter the shop—and she described the display to him in great detail.

"Chipped chamber pots and old boots!" exclaimed Jeremiah. "How can a man make money in such a way? He must be a fool!"

For generations, the Ratchet family in Pagus Parvus had profited from the poor unfortunates in the village. By stealth,

force, and inherited duplicity Jeremiah had continued the tradition. He had acquired ownership of cottages and land, which he rented out to the villagers at rates that could only be described as criminal. He evicted them periodically, to show them he meant business, and then allowed them back on the understanding that they owed him even more rent. Obadiah was not the only one who had made the mistake of falling into debt to him, and in this way Jeremiah's fortune grew.

In his own mind it was all down to his skill as a businessman. Of course, it is easy to be a skilled businessman when there is no competition, but Jeremiah was beginning to realize that Joe might be the rival he had never had. Unfortunately for Jeremiah, he did not own Joe's shop, a fact that caused him immense irritation. What galled him even more than that was Joe's apparent wealth. He had convinced himself that it was Joe's money that afforded him his elevated status, especially as he was so generous with it, and that it couldn't last. Two weeks after the pawnbroker first opened up Jeremiah was surprised to find that Joe's shop was still in business, and judging by the number of people who passed Jeremiah's house on their way up the hill, Joe's foolish trade in chamber pots and old boots was thriving.

Jeremiah was further irked when Obadiah Strang had come up to him in the street with a queer look on his face.

"Now, Obadiah," Jeremiah had said impatiently, "I hope you aren't going to try to get out of this week's rent again. I told you—"

"Here," said Obadiah triumphantly, "take this." He thrust a leather bag toward Jeremiah, who took it and opened it curiously. It was full of coins.

"It's all there," said Obadiah. "Now my debt is paid."

The gravedigger walked away with head held high and Jeremiah stood in the snow, mouth agape. As the passersby began to snigger at him he turned and hurried home. Polly came up from the kitchen and met him in the hall.

"Someone left this for you," she said. She was holding the wooden spade. Jeremiah snorted and pushed past her and went into the study. He slammed the door so hard the windows rattled.

Obadiah wasn't the only one to have suddenly come into money. At least three other debtors had paid up. "Where are they getting it from?" Jeremiah asked himself, and the only answer he could think of was Joe Zabbidou. Jeremiah's temper was now even shorter, and Polly and the stable boy bore the brunt of it. He had never considered that any of them would pay their debts. If business continued in this manner Jeremiah was going to have to find other ways of making money.

Recently he had heard there was profit to be made from selling teeth, both false and real. Ironically, the rich suffered with tooth rot more than the poor. Doubtless their sweeter, more exotic diet was to blame, unlike the coarse fare of their poorer counterparts. Well-off ladies and gentlemen would pay handsomely for a set of real teeth to fill their gaps, not least because it was an obvious show of wealth. Jeremiah

wondered if he could take advantage of this business opportunity. Last time he was in the Nimble Finger he had heard mention of a certain Barton Gumbroot who knew more about these things. Mentally he made a note to meet with him next time he was in the City.

For now, though, he had to deal with the pawnbroker. Every time he thought of Joe, that string bean of a character whose hair defied description, he could feel his teeth clamping together and a headache starting at the base of his neck. As for the boy, his skinny, short-legged attendant who went with him everywhere, he seemed a sly little devil. He wore a scarf and gloves that looked suspiciously like his own, the ones Jeremiah was certain the coach driver had stolen. And those big dark eyes. Jeremiah had never once managed to hold Ludlow's gaze. He always had to look away.

Ever since their first meeting a creeping sense of dissatisfaction had wormed its way into Jeremiah's veins. Now when he walked down the street the villagers looked at him sideways and it unnerved him. His ears were filled with the sound of laughter, though the faces around him were grim. There was a change in the village. It was in the very air he breathed. He could feel it in his bones and it made him shiver. And he knew that it was something to do with the pawnbroker.

It didn't take Jeremiah long to notice Joe's nocturnal visitors. Now what was that all about? Lying awake in the middle of the night, Jeremiah tossed and turned in his foreign-made four-poster bed. The slightest noise seemed to

be magnified tenfold as he listened for the footsteps passing under his window. He had tried to ignore them, burying his face in the mattress, but he couldn't stand the smell of his own breath and had to come up for air. He sat up and frowned and talked to himself and drummed his fingers on the counterpane until he heard the soft crunch of the snow outside on the pavement. Then he would jump from his bed and race to the window. He could see the dark figures going up to Joe's, but he couldn't make out who they were. Whatever it was they were up to, it could only mean more trouble for him. In his nightshirt Jeremiah shook his clenched fist at them and pounded the floor in a fury.

"This man must be stopped," he shouted into the night.

CHAPTER TWENTY

FRAGMENT FROM
THE MEMOIRS OF LUDLOW FITCH

If Joe was a source of interest to the villagers, then I was equally a source of interest to the younger members—namely Polly and the Sourdoughs. I'd not had friends before, and where I came from, people's only loyalty was to money. But the Sourdough boys weren't like that. They were good company and made me laugh and I liked them. Except perhaps for the oldest. I always had the feeling that I couldn't quite trust him. You never really knew what he was thinking.

Polly, however, was less interested in Saluki and more interested in stories from my past. "Tell me about the City," she urged. "I want to know everything."

So I told her: about the dark, enclosed streets with the houses so close together that the sun could never break through; about the broken pavements littered with rotting food, dead animals, dogs, and putrefying rats; about the pools of rancid water and the swarms of flies that hovered in clouds above the surface. I told her about the people, sitting

in the gutter and begging for money to go into the taverns, or lying drunk, thrown out of the same; and I told her about the unbearable coldness of the winter, when people and animals died and froze where they lay.

Through all of this flows the River Foedus, her slow-moving waters thick as soup. Lord but she lives up to her name; her unrelenting stench hangs over the City like a shroud. She is not to be trusted. I have seen her shiver to shrug off the ships tied at the piers, causing them to rock violently from side to side, their creaking and groaning of protest mingling with the frightened shouts of the oarsmen and passengers on the small ferries crossing her broad back. All fear her murky waters. Few are known to have survived such a noxious dipping. And once she has them the Foedus does not surrender her victims quickly. She drags them under and sucks the life out of them, before disgorging them days later bloated with lethal gases and bug-eyed, ready to explode.

The Foedus splits the City in half and divides the people in two. The rich live on her north bank, the poor on the south. One bridge alone spans her back. Perhaps once it had a name but now it is known simply as the Bridge. It is lined on either side with taverns and inns and hostels of the vilest kind, and in these dark and smoky dens of vice all men, whether from the north or the south, are equal: They fight, they gamble, they drink, they murder. I, too, have been in the Nimble Finger Inn, the tavern so beloved of Jeremiah Ratchet and Ma and Pa.

And in a city whose lifeblood is crime, there is also punishment to stem its flow. It's an ill wind that blows no good, and although I hate to say it now, I made a good living then out of the misdeeds of others, especially on a Wednesday: hanging day at Gallows Corner.

A hanging was as good as a holiday. The crowds enjoyed the spectacle almost as much as the poor fellow on the gibbet detested it. The prisoner would arrive on the back of a cart, having been taken from Irongate Prison and driven down Melancholy Lane to the gallows. He would have been in a sorry state when the journey began, but by the end he was wretched. It was common for the onlookers to pelt the cart with whatever came to hand as it passed: rotten fruit and vegetables from the gutters, occasionally a dead cat. I never once threw even a potato peeling at any of those poor devils. Who was to say it wouldn't be me next week?

The crowd cheered as the criminal was led up the steps and the noose was placed around his (or as often as not, her) neck. Now I turned away, not least because this was prime pickpocketing time. When the crowd stood fixated on the ghastly scene unfolding before them I moved among them, taking whatever I could get my hands on. I heard the trapdoor open and the crossbeam creak as the weight fell. And as the crowd roared I sneaked away before anyone noticed that their purse was gone.

Polly lapped up every word. "One day I will go there," she said, her eyes shining. And no matter what I said I couldn't persuade her otherwise.

Although I told Polly many things I didn't tell her about Ma and Pa. I didn't tell her how they robbed me and whipped me or why I really left the City. And I never once said what they had tried to do to me and how it came back to me at night in my dreams. Always my father's face looming above mine and his hands around my neck, or were mine around his?

I could never forgive Ma and Pa for what they did, but I was also grateful to them. Pickpockets, regardless of their age, were treated harshly by the courts. If Ma and Pa hadn't chased me from the City, I know sooner or later the noose would have been around my neck and my lifeless body would have been hanging from those gallows.

CHAPTER TWENTY ONE

Stirling Oliphaunt

As the days wore on more and more villagers were benefiting not only from Joe's generous payments for their pawned goods, but also from his midnight trade. Although they didn't talk about their good fortune, it was obvious that something was afoot. Without a doubt Joe was the breath of fresh air the village had needed for a long, long time. The place seemed brighter somehow, as if the buildings themselves had released a huge sigh and relaxed back to allow the light in. One morning the whole street was brought to a standstill when the clouds parted for a minute or two and blue sky was seen in between.

"It's a miracle," declared Ruby Sourdough. Of course, the clouds came over again and the blue sky was gone, but it was enough to know that it did exist.

Whether this was a miracle or not, the one person in the village who was actually qualified to make such a statement was still in bed and missed the historic event.

The Reverend Stirling Oliphaunt.

For twenty years Stirling Oliphaunt had looked at himself in the mirror every morning (usually not far off noon) and congratulated himself on his posting to Pagus Parvus. A man of his ilk couldn't have asked for a better job—his ilk being that of a lazy, slovenly boor whose purported belief in higher powers furnished him with an easy living. When he had arrived in the village two decades ago he had stood at the gates to the church and cast a bushy-browed, fat-rimmed eye down the hill.

This is what I have been waiting for, he thought. *That hill must be forty degrees, if not more.*

In those days the villagers were a little more inclined to listen to the word of the Lord, so much to Stirling's disappointment, for nearly eight months he was forced to preach a sermon every Sunday. His distinct monotone and the repetitive nature of his subject (the devil, the Dark Side, hell, fire, brimstone, and all related issues) ensured that he addressed an ever-dwindling audience. Eventually, as was his desire, it dwindled to none. Henceforth Stirling passed his days restfully, enjoying fine wines and good food at the church's expense and generally doing as he wished, which was very little. He still thought of God. There had to be one, for how else could a man be blessed with such good fortune?

Now Stirling was more than a little disconcerted by the events of the past few weeks. From his exalted position at the top of the hill, he had not failed to notice the increase in pedestrian traffic. At first he thought the villagers might be coming to him, expecting a service of some kind, and he breathed a sigh of relief when he realized that Joe Zabbidou was the draw.

Stirling had grown used to a life of ease with little interruption and certainly no demands from his flock. When Jeremiah had approached him with the body-snatching business plan Stirling saw no reason to stand in his way, and he was handsomely rewarded with gifts from Jeremiah's wine cellar. This might not strike you as characteristic of Jeremiah until you consider that he drank most of his donations when he came to see Stirling on Thursdays.

Stirling had seen Joe Zabbidou, and his young assistant, that first morning in the graveyard, but he was not inclined to welcome formally the new members of his congregation. Later Polly, who came up every day to cook and clean by arrangement with Jeremiah, told him that the hat shop had a new owner.

"A hatter?" asked the reverend.

"No, a pawnbroker."

"A pawnbroker?"

Polly didn't reply. Stirling had a tendency to turn statement to question—it helped enormously when you didn't have any answers. He had developed the habit in a previous parish where the locals were an inquisitive bunch who enjoyed lively theological debate and were determined that Stirling should enjoy it, too.

"A pawnbroker?" he repeated. He considered briefly how this might affect his position in the village and concluded that it wouldn't affect him at all. In fact, he didn't think Joe's arrival would have much of an effect on anyone. He was surprised, therefore, at the level of animosity Jeremiah Ratchet felt toward the newcomer.

It was late afternoon and the reverend was dozing in a chair when he was brought rapidly back to wakefulness by a tremendous thumping at the door. Polly was there to open it, but she was elbowed out of the way as Jeremiah strode past her into the drawing room.

"Jeremiah?" said Stirling. "A pleasure, I'm sure. Is it Thursday already?"

"It's Tuesday, but I have an important matter to discuss with you."

"Is it about Obadiah and the bodies?"

"Not Obadiah. That blasted pawnbroker."

Stirling roused himself to an upright position.

"Mr. Sobbi—whatever his name is? Isn't he a harmless chap?"

"Harmless!" spluttered Jeremiah. "Harmless! The man is the devil incarnate."

Exhausted by his outburst, and the trip up the hill, Jeremiah fell into the chair opposite the reverend. Polly handed him a drink, topped off Stirling's, and then made herself scarce. It did not do to stay in the same room as that pair. She much preferred to listen from outside the door.

Jeremiah finished his glass in one gulp. He reached over to the table and took the decanter and set it on the hearth beside him.

"Stirling," he announced, "that pawnbroker is very bad for business. In particular, my business. He has filled his window with the greatest collection of junk you have ever seen, and not only that, he has paid for it."

"How is this a problem?" Stirling was trying to sound interested, but he had the beginnings of a headache and was overcome by the urge to yawn.

"His payments are so wildly out of keeping with the true value of the pledges that I fear soon *all* the villagers will be able to pay off their debts."

"I see," said Stirling.

"And if people aren't in debt to me how then do I make money?" continued Jeremiah, and to emphasize his point fully he leaned over and gave Stirling a poke with his fat forefinger. "You have got to do something. My livelihood depends on it."

Now Stirling was awake. "Me? Do something? What can I do?"

"You must convince those peasants that Joe Zabbidou is the devil's spawn."

"The devil's pawn? But is this true?" Stirling had never before thought he might have to deal with the devil's pawn.

"Pawn, spawn," said Jeremiah with intense irritation. "What's the truth got to do with it? This is business. They are to have no further doings with him upon pain of death."

"I'm not sure," said Stirling cautiously.

"Just do it," snapped Jeremiah.

CHAPTER TWENTY-TWO

Stirling Makes a Stand

"Good people of Pagus Parvus," began Stirling, "I beseech of you to listen to me."

Beseech of? he thought in a sudden panic. *Is that right?* No matter, it would do. There was no one here who was an expert in the complexities of the English language. His voice quavered audibly and his hands shook. He wished he had taken a second shot of whisky to steady his nerves. It had been years since he had addressed a crowd, and certainly never in such uncomfortable surroundings. It was snowing lightly and he was standing on a box in the middle of the main street, just north of Jeremiah's house. He had thought it a good spot. He cleared his throat and raised his voice.

"For I tell you now, I have been visited by an angel in the night."

Until this point his audience had consisted of three mortals, namely the Sourdough boys armed and ready with snowballs. Everyone else, once they had established who he was, had walked around him, so much so that his podium was already circled by a ring of footprints in the trampled-down snow. It was only when he said the word *angel* that people stopped to listen. These heavenly creatures appealed greatly to their starved imaginations. Soon there was a small crowd gathered before him, their red-nosed faces looking up at him expectantly.

"An angel?" inquired one.

"Yes, an angel."

"You sure about that, Stirling?" shouted Horatio. "Maybe it was a visitation from the bottle. Too much port can have that effect."

The reverend reddened and carried on. "A great angel came from the clouds and roused me from my bed."

"What did this angel say?" mocked Horatio, making no attempt to disguise his disbelief.

"He said, 'Stirling, you must tell the people of Pagus Parvus to beware, for the devil has come among you and he is tricking you with his wiles and his filthy lucre.'"

"'Wiles and filthy lucre'?" laughed Elias Sourdough. "What language does he speak? Is this angel from a foreign country?"

"Money," said Stirling impatiently. "The devil is among us and luring us with his money."

"There's only one devil in this town and we don't see his money," said Job Wright, the blacksmith, and he pointed in the direction of Jeremiah's house. At the same moment the upstairs curtain twitched, and Stirling wondered if perhaps he should have gone a little farther up the hill.

"Not Mr. Ratchet," he hissed, then raised his voice, "but Joe Zabbidou, the Devil's Pawnbroker." He said this with great feeling, at the same time shaking his clenched fist at the sky. There were gasps all around and Stirling realized that finally he had their full attention. Unwilling to lose this advantage, he hurried along.

"Joe Zabbidou has come to us without warning, appearing from nowhere in the night, to entice you all into his shop with his fancy goods."

Ludlow, who was watching all this from Horatio's doorway, raised his eyebrow. "Fancy goods? A chipped chamber pot. Hardly."

"What does he intend to do with us?" asked Lily Weaver.

"What does he intend to do with us?" repeated Stirling out of habit.

He had not anticipated this question when he had been preparing his speech. He had not thought that he might be challenged. He couldn't recall such a thing when he was in church; granted, most people were asleep then.

The silence was deafening.

"Erm, well, let me see, ah yes, once he has lured you he will take you over to his side, the Dark Side."

Unfortunately for Stirling, this was where he lost his tenuous hold on the audience. Pagus Parvians did not consider the Dark Side in any way threatening. They had not forgotten those long Sunday sermons from years ago when the reverend bored them half to death droning on about the very same subject. They began to shuffle their feet and talk to

their neighbor or walk away. Desperately Stirling tried to re-capture the moment. Jeremiah had promised him a case of the best port.

"If you go over to the Dark Side, then you will be lost for-ever and will burn in the fires of hell."

"At least we'd be warm," shouted Obadiah, and the crowd laughed.

"Do not jest about the Devil," warned Stirling, in a final at-tempt to hold them. "You never know when he is listening."

"Hang about, Reverend," said Ruby Sourdough. "Here comes the beast himself. Why don't we ask him about this Dark Side?"

Joe was indeed coming down the street at his usual jaunty pace. He had the grip of a mountain goat. Right now one or two of the villagers were wondering whether his shoes did indeed conceal those telltale cloven feet.

"'Morning, all," he called and smiled. "Did I hear some-one mention my name?"

Although Stirling was not being taken seriously, it did seem to some a rather curious coincidence that Joe had turned up at this particular moment.

"'Ere, listen to this, Mr. Zabbidoof," said the youngest Sourdough, at the front of the crowd. "Stirling says yore the Devil come 'ere to burn us all in 'ell."

Stirling protested immediately. It had never been his in-tention to actually confront Beelzebub, merely to slander him in his absence. "I didn't say that," he protested hurriedly. "It is a sin to tell a lie, lad."

"Yes 'e did," said Elias Sourdough to Joe. "'E said you were gonna loor us wiv your tricks and wiles."

Joe smiled. "I have no tricks. You know what I am, a pawn-broker. Have I ever pretended or acted otherwise? As for wiles, you are welcome to come and look for them. Perhaps they are in the window?"

At that everyone burst into raucous laughter. Stirling scowled, picked up his box, and slunk away.

CHAPTER TWENTY-THREE

FRAGMENT FROM
THE MEMOIRS OF LUDLOW FITCH

Stirling's performance in the street was the talk of the villagers for three whole days. As far as they were concerned, the reverend's humiliation was just one more in the eye for Mr. Ratchet (who had watched the entire scene from his window, barely concealed behind the curtain) and another victory for Mr. Zabbidou. The battle lines might as well have been drawn in the snow.

There was no disputing Pagus Parvus had given Joe a warm welcome. It could be measured almost from the moment he defied Jeremiah Ratchet. This initial enthusiasm had not waned—just the opposite—it had increased immensely. Now at the very sight of him the villagers behaved as if he were royalty. I swear upon my evil pa that I witnessed more than once some fellow kneeling before him. Poor Joe, he could not go from one end of the street to the other without being stopped a dozen times by well-wishers, inquiring after his health and his business and even Saluki.

Joe was always polite. His manner was consistently warm and friendly, but I could tell that this adulation was beginning to trouble him.

"I did not come here to be venerated," he mumbled.

As I lay during long sleepless nights the same question turned over in my mind: "What did you come here for?" I knew by now that things were not, and could not be, as simple as they appeared. A man arrives out of nowhere in an isolated village and hands over money from a bottomless source for worthless objects and secrets. It didn't make sense to me, but whenever I tried to ask Joe about his past he refused to engage and immediately talked about something else.

I wondered whether Joe's aversion to all the attention was modesty, and I paid little notice to his discomfort. While he tried to avoid the limelight, I bathed in his reflected glory. When I walked the streets of the City I was nobody: In Pagus Parvus I was prince to Joe's king. Of course, Joe was the one they wanted to talk to, his was the hand they wished to shake, but they spoke to me, too, if only to say good morning. It made me smile. If they had ever seen me in the City they would have crossed to the other side of the road.

Perhaps it was the fact that the village was so isolated that made Joe (and me) even more special. But, special or not, I had a feeling that as long as Jeremiah Ratchet was in Pagus Parvus it wasn't going to be enough.

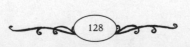

Our days were always busy. I had my jobs to do and Joe had his, but we were never rushed. Being in the shop sometimes felt like being in another world where everything happened at half speed. I never saw Joe make a hurried movement; there was no urgency to his life, but, for all that, it was difficult to shake off the feeling that we were waiting for something to happen.

In the late afternoon, when it was quiet and Polly and the Sourdoughs would have been and gone, we would both sit by the fire and enjoy the warmth and the comfort it brought. At such times I couldn't imagine ever returning to the City.

"I'm never going back," I said to Joe one night.

"Never say never," Joe replied quickly. "All things change."

Certainly my fortunes had changed. In my eyes Joe was the father I had always wished for. I had new clothes that he had given me. As for my rags, we both enjoyed watching them burn on the fire that night. At least once a fortnight I relaxed in front of the fire in a huge tin tub filled to the brim with hot water, and every day we had two decent meals. The Pagus Parvians had proved most hospitable and hardly a day passed without some sort of food parcel being left on the doorstep: rabbits, pigeons, sparrows (a delicacy in these parts, marvelous stuffed with onion and allium) and occasionally a whole chicken from the butcher's.

"Bribes." Joe laughed. "They think if they feed me I will change my mind." He didn't, but he still threw the meat in the pot.

As the harsh memories of my previous life faded, my mind started to play strange tricks on me. I began to worry that life was too good. Surely a boy such as I, with my past and the crimes I had committed, deserved punishment, not reward?

Joe tried to reassure me. "It's common enough to think like that," he said, "to feel unworthy of good fortune, but have you forgotten what I said to you about luck?"

"You said we make our own luck."

"Exactly. You made yours by coming here. Now you work hard and you deserve what you have."

"But I never intended to come here," I insisted. "It was chance that Ratchet's carriage was outside the Nimble Finger."

"But it was you who chose Jeremiah's carriage."

"What if I had gone down the hill instead of up? I might have worked with Job Wright shoeing horses. Then you would have taken on one of the Sourdough boys when they came up to see the frog."

"That is a possibility," said Joe, "but the Sourdough boys can barely read or write."

"I can only do that because I went to Mr. Jellico."

"But you sought him out."

And so it would go on, in circles, until one evening Joe asked, "Are you happy here?"

"Yes."

"And if you could go back in time, to the City, what would you change?"

"I don't know," I said. "If I had done something different then I might never have met you."

"Exactly," said Joe with finality. "Everything that happened to you, bad or otherwise, ultimately brought you here."

There the conversation ended because the shop door opened and someone called for service. Joe always woke at the sound of the door, no matter how deeply asleep he seemed, but in case he didn't Saluki gave a violent belch whenever she heard someone approaching. I felt it was a warning.

For a frog, Saluki was good company. When I had the chance I liked to feed her, to watch her tongue shoot out across the length of the tank, and almost too quick to see, the bug or grub or insect would be gone. I had not taken the lid off the tank again since that first day. Joe had forbidden me to do so and I didn't want to touch her. Occasionally he took her out and held her in the palm of his hand. He would stroke her back with such gentleness, and she would burp softly and seem to glow. I hadn't forgotten what he had said about gaining her trust, and I hoped that one day I would.

I remember those days in the shop well, warm and cozy away from the cold outside world. But of course the outside world still came knocking at the door. The villagers were obviously grateful for everything Joe had done for them, and gradually, one by one, they were freeing themselves from Jeremiah's iron grip. But their previous desperation was now replaced by anger—that Jeremiah had treated them so badly

for so long, that he had taken so much from them, that he had kept them living in fear. As each managed to pay Jeremiah back the money they owed, they wished to pay him back in other ways, too.

One night we had a visit from the local physician, Dr. Samuel Mouldered. I wasn't surprised. After all, Joe had sought him out the previous day, as he did all his midnight customers, and invited him up. Like most, he had an interesting tale to tell.

Samuel Mouldered was a rather morbid man with a permanently gloomy expression on his face, so his patients never knew if they were to live or die. They may have been alarmed to discover that often the doctor did not know, either. You see, Mouldered wasn't a doctor at all, just a convincing quack who was on the run from a posse of duped customers who had discovered that his miracle cure was little more than boiled nettles and corked wine.

Pagus Parvus was an ideal hiding place for such a man. To be fair, Mouldered was quite harmless. Since coming to the village some ten years ago he had practiced medicine on the premise that most illnesses burned themselves out over the course of seven days. Thus he prescribed his miracle cure (now a more palatable mixture of honey and beer) for a week's duration, and on the whole he achieved quite remarkable results. As for death itself, no one ever questioned the unusually high occurrence of heart attacks in the area. They trusted the doctor and his diagnoses.

Samuel Mouldered's greatest fear was that Jeremiah would discover his secret.

"I cannot promise that Jeremiah will never find out," Joe had said, "but he will not hear it from us. You have my word."

Joe held the door open, but Mouldered seemed reluctant to go.

"The man is a monster," he declared. "For years we have suffered at his hands. The villagers want revenge. I know they hope you will help them."

"What can I do?" asked Joe quietly. "I am merely a pawnbroker."

"That's not what they think," muttered the doctor as he stepped into the street. Joe merely shrugged and handed Dr. Mouldered a purse of coins.

"*Vincit qui patitur,*" called Joe after him, but he was already out of earshot.

I looked at him.

"Who waits, wins."

I listened to Dr. Mouldered's confession, writing it all down as was my duty, but I was uneasy. I asked Joe again if he didn't think we should do something.

"People's lives might be in danger," I said. "Dr. Mouldered doesn't know what he is doing."

Joe was adamant. "He's not doing any harm. And there is no one else in the village who would do his job."

I protested some more and Joe had to remind me that we were in the business of keeping secrets.

"How long do you think we would last if we gave away this information? The business would be in ruins."

The business, I thought. *What business?* We certainly weren't making a profit. Surely the money had to run out eventually and what would happen then? But I had slipped into this way of life so easily and I couldn't bear the thought that it might change, so I kept my doubts to myself because, whether or not I understood what was going on, I was unwilling to do anything that might upset Joe.

CHAPTER TWENTY-FOUR

Jeremiah Has a Plan

Jeremiah Ratchet was close to his wits' end. He had had just about enough of Joe Zabbidou's apparent disregard for his standing in the community. His business, his lifestyle, his pleasures were all in jeopardy because of that man. He could hardly bring himself to say Joe's name and even then he could only spit it, usually accompanied by a shower of brown, stringy saliva and crumbs. Jeremiah liked to mull things over at dinner.

Jeremiah rarely ate in his magnificent dining room and usually took his meals in the study with a dinner tray on his lap. It was a room of generous proportions, though badly lit, and shelved from floor to ceiling. Each shelf was packed tightly, bowing under the weight of an extensive array of books. Jeremiah was a collector. He loved to have things, sometimes for no other reason than that. He was not much of a reader, mind; he found the concentration required quite a strain on his head. As a rule he only kept books that he thought would impress others or increase in price. As a result the titles tended to be obscure and either full of facts that he didn't understand or plots that he couldn't fathom. Jeremiah was a fine example of the sort of person who knew the cost of everything but the value of nothing.

In his study Jeremiah bit into a mouthful of lamb and chewed thoughtfully on Joe Zabbidou. The man was a complete menace. Earlier that day Job Wright had come up to Jeremiah outside the baker's and presented him with a purse of money that covered over half his debt. Then, after lunch, Polly told Jeremiah about the pair of horseshoes she had seen in the pawnbroker's window, and Jeremiah knew that once again Joe Zabbidou had been at work.

"They're lovely and shiny," Polly had said innocently. "I should imagine Joe paid very good money for them." She left the room quickly and Jeremiah was certain he heard her sniggering all the way to the kitchen.

"I should have thrown him out that very first day," he said ruefully. "I left it too late." But even Jeremiah suspected that it would never have been that easy.

Jeremiah realized, of course, that his tenants' sudden ability to pay was directly linked to the display in the pawnbroker's window. He reckoned, however, that Joe could not possibly finance everyone's debt and that sooner or later he would be out of business and then everything would be back

to normal. But Joe did not operate within the usual constraints of commerce.

Jeremiah shook his head slowly. "How can a man thrive when he pays a small fortune for worthless junk?" he asked himself every day. And every day he waited for Polly to come back from the Reverend Stirling's so he could hear the latest report on the shop window. And every day it plunged him deeper into depression. How it had pained him to call upon Stirling for help when he had proved to be little better than useless.

"What shall I do?" moaned Jeremiah as he saw his income dwindling further, for once all the arrears were paid, he couldn't possibly survive on rent alone.

He still had money in the bank, inherited from his father, but it had been greatly depleted over the years by his frequent gambling. Jeremiah's high living had a price. He owed money to his tailor and his hat maker, to his wig maker and his boot maker, and he preferred not to think of the debts that were mounting at the card table.

There was blackmail, of course. Since he had unearthed Horatio's little secret there had been no shortage of fresh meat in his kitchen. And until recently he had been making good money from Obadiah and the grave robbing. Unfortunately, as far as grave robbing was concerned, things weren't looking too good at present, and not only Joe was to blame. Jeremiah's bodysnatchers (who also doubled up as bailiffs during the day when Jeremiah needed help with

an eviction) had brought him the bad news a couple of nights ago.

"The anatomists in the City don't want the old bodies no more," said one of the bodysnatchers. "They want fresh young ones."

Jeremiah groaned. "Don't they understand? There aren't any young corpses in Pagus Parvus."

"It doesn't have to be a problem," said the other man carefully.

"How do you mean?" asked Jeremiah.

The wily pair exchanged knowing glances, which was not easy through their black face masks, and burst into throaty laughter. "Well, let's just say there's a young lad up the hill, in the old hat shop, would make a nice specimen."

"Ludlow?" asked Jeremiah. "But he's alive and kicking."

"The fresher the better," said the first.

For a fleeting moment Jeremiah actually considered just what they were suggesting. Many times he had wished never to have to meet Ludlow's knowing gaze again, but as a solution to his problems, out-and-out murder was a little extreme even for Jeremiah.

"No, no," said Jeremiah hurriedly. "I'm sure that won't be necessary. There must be another way. What about teeth?"

"Teeth?"

"I heard you can sell them," began Jeremiah, but the two men just laughed. "Oh, never mind," he ended despondently.

The men shrugged in unison. "Then there's nothing else

we can do for you. Give us our money and we'll trouble you no more."

And that had been that.

Jeremiah set aside his plate, the meal only half eaten, and slouched back into his chair. He had no appetite. He was too depressed to look at his books, not even *The Loneliness of the High Mountain Shepherd*—his all-time favorite, on account of the fact that shepherds tended to have a limited vocabulary and to tell a simple story.

If Joe stayed in the village and continued as he had done up until now, Jeremiah knew that it could only mean more trouble for him. He was going to have to take matters into his own hands.

"Pagus Parvus is not big enough for the two of us," he declared to the shadows. "One of us will have to go."

Feeling very sorry for himself, he trudged upstairs and prepared for bed. He couldn't resist looking out of the window. By now it was an obsession. He could see the pawnbroker's shop at the top of the hill and the smoke that curled out of the chimney every night into the early hours.

"What is he doing up there?" he asked himself for the hundredth time.

Jeremiah was still no nearer to finding out why the pawnbroker received visitors well into the night, and he lacked the imagination to come up with an explanation on his own. He had heard someone say that Joe was giving advice, but he could discover no more. He asked Polly many times if she knew what it was all about, but she just looked at him blankly.

If only I could find out, thought Jeremiah, *then perhaps I might be able to do something.* But whatever nighttime trade was going on at the pawnbroker's, no one would talk about it. So Jeremiah drew his own conclusions and decided that it was all part of Joe's plot against him. Having concluded thus, he was even more desperate to know the truth. One morning, therefore, when the oldest Sourdough dropped off the bread, Jeremiah was waiting for him outside the kitchen door and grabbed him by the scruff of the neck.

"I want you to do a little job for me," Ratchet muttered.

"Does it pay?" asked the boy.

Jeremiah laughed and the poor lad was treated to a panoramic view of the inside of his mouth. That mottled tongue, the fleshy uvula, those stained teeth, the meat and piecrust from the previous night still wedged firmly between them.

"I'll tell you what you'll get if you don't do it," he hissed. "I'll tell your father that I found you sneaking around my kitchen looking for something to steal. Something like this," and with a sleight of hand that would have surprised even Joe, Jeremiah somehow managed to take a silver candlestick out of the boy's pocket, upon which trick the poor chap burst into tears.

Jeremiah released his hold. "Just do what I say," he growled, "and you'll be no worse off. You must find out what's going on at the pawnbroker's."

The lad hesitated, but the threat of his father was enough. He really had no choice. It took him a week, standing hour after hour in the freezing cold at midnight around the back of the pawnbroker's shop. And every night it was the same. He heard the crunch of snow and the knock at the door. He watched as Joe handed his visitor a drink and sat him by the fire. In the corner he could see Ludlow writing furiously in a large black book. He could not hear what was being said, but he guessed quite quickly what was in the leather bags that Joe handed over at the end of the meeting. Eventually he decided he had learned as much as he was going to (he was also becoming increasingly afraid that Joe had seen him), and duly presented himself in Jeremiah's study.

"So?" asked Jeremiah eagerly. "What did you find out?"

"They talk to Joe and Ludlow writes down what they say in a big black book."

"And that's it?" It wasn't at all what Jeremiah expected.

The boy nodded. "Whatever they're telling him, it's worth money. Joe pays them, bags of it. Dr. Mouldered was there the other night. I couldn't quite hear what he was saying, but his face looked as if it might be important. And I know my own father has been up there."

So did Jeremiah. Elias Sourdough had paid him nearly all his back rent.

"And what of the frog?" asked Jeremiah in desperation. He couldn't see how any of this was going to help him.

"She's called Saluki. Joe treats her like she's something special. He won't let anyone touch her, but sometimes she

sits in his hand. I reckon she might be worth a few shillings. I've never seen anything like her."

Jeremiah was perplexed. As he lay in bed that night thinking over what he had been told, it gradually dawned on him that, in fact, the Sourdough boy had given him exactly what he needed to know.

"The book," he said out loud and sat bolt upright. "The book holds the answer."

Jeremiah's mind was racing. Whatever was in that book, Joe was prepared to pay handsomely for it. It made sense then that if Joe somehow lost the book, or perhaps it was taken from him, then he would also pay handsomely to retrieve it. Or, better than that, perhaps he would agree to leave Pagus Parvus *and* pay up in order to get the book back. With Joe gone, all Jeremiah's problems would be solved. Jeremiah's excitement mounted. What a fine revenge he could exact for all the trouble Joe had caused him. But there was one small flaw in the plan.

How do I get the book in the first place? he wondered. But just before sunrise he had the answer. The time had come for Jeremiah Ratchet to pay Joe Zabbidou a visit.

CHAPTER TWENTY FIVE

The Cat's Away

Ludlow stirred. A log split on the fire beside him and a new flame burst from its heart. He welcomed the warmth. Joe had long since reclaimed his cloak.

"One day you will have a cloak such as this, Ludlow," he had said, "but it must be earned. Jocastar wool does not come cheap."

Joe had not left him lacking. In the place of the cloak he had given Ludlow a large cushion stuffed with straw and two rough but clean-smelling blankets. Every night Ludlow curled up on the cushion and covered himself right up to his ears with the blankets.

But sleep did not come easy, and when he did sleep his vivid dreams caused him to twitch and mutter. More often than not he woke in a sweat after some strange dream about one of the villagers. Jeremiah, smelling so badly that Ludlow would wrinkle his nose as he slept; Obadiah, always in a hole, always digging; Horatio mixing the ingredients for one of his vile pies. The confessions of the Pagus Parvians would haunt him until the dream would turn into a nightmare. The villagers would recede into a sort of fog and his father's face would suddenly appear above him. His hands would reach out of the mist and tighten around Ludlow's neck until everything went black. Then he would wake up violently and leave his bed to look out of the window down the street until he was driven back by the cold.

Every morning Joe would ask, "How did you sleep?" and every morning Ludlow gave the same reply, "Well, very well indeed." Joe would raise a skeptical eyebrow but he never said more.

One morning, after a particularly bad night, when Ludlow had been shaken awake five times by the hands throttling him, Joe announced he was to be away for a few days.

"You needn't open the shop if you prefer," he said. "The weather feels quite stormy. I doubt there'd be much customers."

Ludlow, although he wanted to appear willing, protested only feebly. He liked the thought of having the place to himself for a while.

"When will you be back?" he asked as Joe stepped out into the street.

"When my business is done."

Ludlow could sense there was little point pursuing the matter, and he watched as his employer limped off up the hill past the graveyard. Joe was right. The skies were ominously dark today and the cobbles were buried under a fresh snowfall. There was little other life in the street, but it was only five o'clock in the morning. As soon as Joe was out of sight Ludlow closed the door and promptly jumped onto Joe's bed and went back to sleep.

When he woke some hours later he thought for a moment that he had slept right through the day and into the night. In fact, it was midafternoon, but it was uncommonly dark and cold. Outside a screaming wind buffeted the walls and windows; inside snow had fallen down the chimney and was gathering on the hearth. The fire had practically gone out and Ludlow knew that he must revive it. When he had finally brought it back to life and had a kettle hanging over the flame he went through to the shop and stood at the door. His view of the street was somewhat obscured, for the village was in the grip of a snowstorm the like of which he had never seen before. The three golden orbs were blowing wildly in the wind and snow was piling up in every corner and doorway. He could see no more than a few feet down the street.

What about Joe? he thought. He could only hope he had found shelter before the storm. Then a flash of red in the white flurries caught his eye. Someone was outside.

"Oh, Lord," muttered Ludlow. "It's Polly." He opened the door and it was snatched out of his hand by the wind. Huge flakes stung his face and he was half blinded by the driving snow.

"Polly!" he shouted. "Polly!"

Polly was almost close enough to touch but she couldn't hear him over the whine of the wind. Ludlow didn't stop to

think and he stepped out into the full force of the storm. He grabbed Polly by the arm and pulled her toward him. Her white face lit up under her hood and together the two of them leaned into the wind and collapsed inside the shop. The door slammed shut behind them.

"What were you doing out there?" cried Ludlow.

Polly answered in short breathless gasps. "I was—coming back—from Stirling Oliphaunt's." She was shivering violently, her nose bright red with the cold. "He doesn't care—about the weather—he still wants me to clean for him."

Ludlow shook his head in disbelief. "You could die out there. You're freezing. Come through and have some soup. The fire's lit. You can stay until the weather clears."

Polly hesitated. She had only been behind the counter once, the night when she confessed to various petty crimes, mainly relating to Jeremiah Ratchet and her pilfering of small knickknacks from his house. Although she felt that she deserved them, and she needed the money, equally she had felt the need to confess.

"Where is he?" she asked, looking around nervously. Polly couldn't help feeling a little scared of Joe Zabbidou, and she was always afraid of what she might say if he looked at her with his cool gray eyes.

Ludlow shook his head. "He's away. I'm in charge."

Polly relaxed a little and followed Ludlow through to the fire, where she stood close enough to be singed but not quite close enough to catch alight. "Mr. Ratchet would kill me if he knew I was in here with you." She laughed. "He don't mind

me spying for him, but he said not to fratter—fratter-something with the two of you."

"Fraternize?" asked Ludlow.

"That's the word."

"What do you mean, spying?" interrupted Ludlow. "So is that why you come?"

"Of course not," said Polly indignantly. "But it gives me a good excuse. Your Mr. Zabbidou has Mr. Ratchet tearing his hair out. Jeremiah wants so badly to know what goes on up here that he's told me to look in the window every day and tell him what I see."

"And what is that?" asked Ludlow stiffly.

"Junk," she replied.

"And?"

She saw the look on Ludlow's face and added quickly, "I don't tell him nothing else. Not even about the book."

"Maybe Jeremiah should come up one night," said Ludlow.

"Ooh, yes, I bet he has a secret or two." Polly moved a little away from the fire and looked directly at Ludlow. "Do you?"

Ludlow frowned. "Me? No. What do you mean?"

"Don't get your pants in a pickle," Polly teased. "I was only asking. I suppose you don't need to sell your secrets, with what Joe pays you."

"Hmm," said Ludlow, thinking of a way to change the subject.

"I told a lie or two when I was up here," said Polly suddenly.

"When Joe said he paid for secrets, I reckoned the worser the secret was, the more money he'd give me." Quickly she put her hand to her mouth and shook her head, annoyed with herself. "I don't know why I told you that. I don't want you to think badly of me." Then she laughed. "Stop looking at me like that, it makes my tongue loose!"

She looked around again, more slowly this time. "So, where is it then?"

"What?" Ludlow wished Polly would stop asking him so many questions.

"The book of secrets. The one you write in."

"It's hidden," he said quickly, but his eyes flicked to Joe's bed before he could help himself. Polly saw and in an instant dived for it. Ludlow lurched toward her but he was too slow. Polly stuck her hand under the mattress and grabbed the Black Book. She pulled it out, jumped onto the bed, and held it out of Ludlow's reach.

"Let's have a look then," she said mischievously, waving it above her head. "There must be some interesting tales in here."

"No," said Ludlow desperately, "it's forbidden. Joe says so."

Polly laughed. "Joe's not here, in case you hadn't noticed. What harm would it do?"

"No," said Ludlow, but with less conviction. After all, it wasn't as if Polly was suggesting something he hadn't already thought of.

"I promised Joe," he said weakly.

"Joe wouldn't know," said Polly slowly. "And you must have heard most of these secrets already."

"Only the ones from Pagus Parvus."

"Then let's look at the others, from before Pagus Parvus, in a place where we don't know anyone. How could that be wrong?"

Ludlow could see how it made sense, probably because he wanted it to. He sat on the bed feeling a crippling twinge of guilt, but ignored it. This was the first time he had been left alone with the Black Book of Secrets, and already he was about to betray Joe. But if he was honest with himself, he wanted to read the stories as much as Polly did.

"I suppose we could look at the beginning."

Polly nodded eagerly. "The very first story, the oldest."

"All right," said Ludlow firmly. "But no more."

"Of course," said Polly. "Here you are then," she said, handing Ludlow the book.

"I thought *you* wanted to do it," said Ludlow, putting his hands behind his back as if by not actually touching the book he wouldn't be part of the betrayal.

"But I can't read, stupid," said Polly matter-of-factly. "We don't all have your fine education."

Ludlow sighed, and unable to hold off any longer, he took the heavy book from Polly's hands. Feeling slightly sick, he slowly opened the cover, smoothed down the very first page, and began.

CHAPTER TWENTY-SIX

EXTRACT FROM
THE BLACK BOOK OF SECRETS

The Coffin Maker's Confession

My name is Septimus Stern and I have an odious secret. It has followed me for nearly twenty years. Wherever I go I know it is there, like a shadow, waiting to pounce on me when I least expect it, to torture me for another night, to make me hate myself even more than I do already.

I am a prisoner of my own mind and you, Mr. Zabbidou, are my last hope of release.

I am a coffin maker by trade, and a fine one at that. Over the years my reputation spread far and wide across the country and I was never short of work. It might seem strange to you that I make my living from the misery of others, but I am not a sentimental man, Mr. Zabbidou. I believe I provide a service to those in need, regardless of the circumstances, and I earn my reward.

Very early one morning, in late autumn, a stranger came

into my workshop. He claimed to be a physician and insisted that I call him Dr. Sturgeon.

"A patient of mine has just died," he said mournfully, "and I need a coffin."

He seemed a little nervous, but that was not unusual. I said that was the business I was in and I was sure I could help him out.

"I have been assured you are a fine coffin maker," he continued. "I want you to do something special for me."

Again, I thought nothing of this request. I presumed he meant that I should line the box in a luxurious material, silk perhaps, or maybe use a more expensive wood. Sometimes I was asked to fit gold or silver handles and plates. All this I had done before and I told him so, but he shook his head.

"No, that is not what I want. You see, you may recall the case recently where a young man was buried while still alive. I hasten to say it was not I who pronounced him dead. You can imagine the distress this caused the family when they subsequently discovered that he had attempted to break free from the coffin and was unable."

I said to Dr. Sturgeon that indeed I did recall the case in question, for I had provided the coffin. The dead man had been placed in the family tomb and a month later, following the death of another family member, they opened the tomb to find the coffin on its side on the floor. They opened the lid, but of course it was too late then. Their son was quite decayed, though it was still clear to see that his hands were

no longer by his sides and, by all accounts, his mouth was open in an expression of excruciating despair.

"I wish to ensure the same tragedy cannot happen again."

I thought this a sensible notion and listened as he outlined his idea for a coffin with a mechanism that allowed air to circulate around it in case the deceased should ever wake up. We agreed on a price, and as speed was of the essence, I started work straight away. It was not a complicated design, requiring little more than a pipe connected to the coffin that should reach the surface to allow air in (the doctor insisted this should be concealed—"It might upset the vicar," he explained), and I completed it late that night. I delivered it myself the next day to the address given, a grand country manor, some hours' horse ride away. The doctor himself opened the door.

"Welcome," he said. "The master is a little indisposed at present. He has asked that I deal with this business."

He beckoned me in and we passed an open door and when I glanced within I saw a man, whom I presumed to be the master, sitting very still in a chair by the window. He was pale and old and looked quite ill. The doctor inspected the coffin thoroughly and asked many questions as to its reliability. Finally, when he was reassured that it would operate efficiently, we carried it down into the cellar.

"It is the master's wife who has died," he said. "She lies in the cellar where it is cool."

"How did she meet her end?" I asked as we struggled with the awkward burden.

"An ague," he said and was no more forthcoming than that.

Finally we reached the bottom. The temperature was considerably lower than upstairs and I saw the lady lying stretched out on a table. She looked pale but peaceful, and contrary to my expectations, there were no signs of sickness. I don't know what it was about the whole affair, but suddenly my suspicions were aroused. She looked so tranquil it was difficult to believe that she was dead, but certainly there were no signs of life. There was a strange smell in the room which at the time I attributed to the dampness.

"Tragic," I murmured.

"It is indeed," replied the doctor, and despite the coolness I saw that he was sweating. He stroked the dead lady's hand with unequaled tenderness and it disturbed me to see how he looked upon her. After all, she was not his wife.

"So young and beautiful," he said. "The vicar is coming over this afternoon and she shall be buried in the family plot."

Once we had deposited the coffin the doctor seemed anxious to show me to the door. "I think perhaps you should delay no longer," he urged. "The weather is turning and the day is wearing on. I should not like to think of you on that road at night. It is notorious for highwaymen."

I inferred from his tone that I had outstayed my welcome, and so I took off there and then. I did not feel that the weather was any worse than that morning, in fact it seemed better, but I was pleased to be gone from the place. I had been well rewarded for my work, but it left me with a nagging doubt that something was not right. For days afterward I could not rid my nostrils of the smell in the cellar.

Some months later by chance I happened to travel to that same region again. An impulse made me take the fork in the road that led to the manor, and I stopped at the gates. They were locked, but through the bars I could see that the house was closed up and the gardens were overgrown. There was a notice on the pillar that the property was up for sale and to contact the agents Messrs. Cruickshank and Butterworth in the next town. As that was my intended destination, I paid a visit to their offices to inquire as to the whereabouts of the owner. I spoke to Mr. Cruickshank, a most affable gentleman, who answered my many inquiries comprehensively.

"Strange affair," he said. "First the wife dies and then the master. Only the son left. He inherited the lot. He's gone abroad and left instructions for us to dispose of the property on his behalf. Should make him a small fortune."

"Son?" I queried.

"Aye, a doctor."

"How did the old man die?" I asked.

"Now that's an even queerer tale. The night after the wife was buried the doctor heard screaming from his father's room. He ran in and found his father half dead in his bed, purple in the face, hardly able to move apparently, barely able to speak. He told the doctor that he had woken to see his dead wife kneeling over him with her hands around his throat, strangling him. He died soon after. The shock killed him—he had a feeble constitution and his heart couldn't

take it. I feel sorry for the son. The poor chap lost a father and a stepmother in one go."

"You mean the dead woman wasn't his mother?"

Mr. Cruickshank shook his head. "His real mother died when he was but a lad and his father married again. She was the prettiest lady I ever did see, though nearly forty years his junior. Don't know what she saw in him myself."

I thanked Mr. Cruickshank for his time and went on my way, but I was even more unsettled than before. My curiosity had been satisfied but my suspicions had not been allayed. As had been my intention all along, I paid a visit to the apothecary to purchase a cough remedy. When I entered the shop I was halted in my tracks by a potent and unmistakable smell. The very same smell I had noticed in the cellar at the manor. When he heard the bell the apothecary came out to see me.

"What is that smell?" I asked without delay.

"Ah," he said conspiratorially, "it is my very own special sleep remedy. Highly effective, very powerful. It sends a person into a deep sleep and once asleep they look quite lifeless and cannot feel pain. I believe the surgeons in the hospitals might find it useful in operations."

"Tell me," I said with a quickening heart, "do you know a Dr. Sturgeon?"

"One of my best customers," he said proudly. "He swore the remedy was the best and only cure for his insomnia."

I took my cough linctus and started for home with a heavy heart. Now I knew the truth of the deception into which I

had been unwittingly dragged. What a convoluted plot. Only the most devilish of minds could have dreamed it up. After all, how can you try a ghost for murder?

You see, Mr. Zabbidou, I believe the young doctor administered the apothecary's potion to his father's wife and tricked his father into believing she had died. Then, with the aid of my coffin, he buried her. While underground she could still breathe, so when the potion wore off and he unearthed her later that night, she was sufficiently alive to appear at her husband's bedside and to half strangle him, knowing that his heart was feeble. So not only did the doctor inherit his estate but also his young wife. Doubtless now the two of them are enjoying the fruits of their wickedness in a far-off country.

I cannot forgive myself for the part I played. You're the only person in the world who knows this, Mr. Zabbidou. I hate to think that anyone else should ever find out what I did. They say you are a man of your word and I believe them. Now I think I can sleep. ✳

CHAPTER TWENTY SEVEN

Fragment from
The Memoirs of Ludlow Fitch

After I finished reading the coffin maker's secret we both looked at each other guiltily.

"Poor beggar," said Polly quietly. "It wasn't even his fault."

"There's a little bit more," I said. "Right at the bottom of the page."

"What does it say?"

"*Quae nocent docent.*"

Polly looked blank.

"I think it must be Latin."

"Latin?"

"It's another language. Joe uses it sometimes. He says you can say more with fewer words. He likes that."

"Well, you'd better not ask him what it means," said Polly quickly, "or he'll know you've been snooping."

I said nothing. I couldn't help feeling Joe would know anyway. I closed the book and put it away.

"I don't want to hear anymore," said Polly and I was glad.

So we sat and waited for the storm to ease. Just the two of us, in front of the fire drinking soup and wrapped in blankets to keep warm. I think we both knew we were wrong to read the book, but Polly tried to shrug it off with a laugh.

"He'll never know," she said, trying to convince herself. "Don't fret so much."

By early evening the wind had died down and the snow had eased. Polly stood up and stretched. "I'll be off," she said. "Mr. Ratchet'll be looking for his supper." Before she went she looked at me nervously.

"You won't tell him, will you, Ludlow?"

I shook my head. "If he finds out, I'll say it was just me."

She grinned. "He'll forgive you. Just stare at him with your big green eyes."

Somehow I didn't think that trick would work on Joe.

Four days later, although the worst of the storm was over, it was still dark and wintry and very cold. I kept the shop locked up. The hours passed slowly. I fed Saluki and swept the floor and dusted the display. I had plenty of time to think about what Polly and I had done, and by the fourth day I had managed to convince myself that I need not have worried. After all, no one had come to any harm. We didn't do it out of malice, just curiosity. At the back of my mind was the nagging doubt that Joe had set a trap for me, and although it hurt me to think that he didn't trust me, it was

worse to know that he was right. But did that make it fair? Was there any person out there strong enough to resist looking?

The night before his return I was nearly asleep by the fire when I thought I heard a noise outside. By the time I opened the door onto the street there was no one there, only footprints under the window, large footprints. I knew who had made them, not from their size but from the smell that lingered in the air. A Jeremiah Ratchet smell.

On the fifth morning Saluki set up a tremendous croaking and a few seconds later someone began rattling at the door. "Ludlow," called a voice, "let me in."

It was Joe. I was very pleased to have him back and I only hoped that I could hide my guilty feelings. He came in, looked the place over, and clapped me on the back.

"Good to see you kept the shop in order in my absence," he said. I had made sure that everything was in its place.

"There was a terrible storm," I said before I could stop myself. "Polly came by and sat with me for a while." I hadn't meant to tell him that, but when Joe looked at me in a certain way I just had to say what was on my mind. I stared at the floor. I didn't want to reveal any more of my thoughts.

"I know," he replied.

"You know?" Had he read my mind?

"I've just seen her in the street, going to the butcher's. She told me all about it."

My heart shuddered. I hoped that was all Polly had said.

"Anyone come knocking?" Joe asked.

I shook my head. "I think Ratchet was sniffing around, though."

"Shouldn't surprise me. He's an inquisitive fellow. He's certainly not the first to spy at the window."

Joe didn't just mean me. I remembered when Dr. Mouldered came up, Joe told me afterward he was certain someone had been outside. But right now I was interested in Ratchet. "Why don't you do something about him" I urged. "Is it really so unreasonable of the villagers to ask?"

Joe sighed. "You must be patient, Ludlow."

"Why? What are we waiting for? Do you know what's ahead?"

This seemed to amuse him. "Have you seen my crystal ball?" he asked. "If you have, I should very much like to know where it is." He was half laughing, but then he became serious again.

"I am no seer, Ludlow, believe me. If I was, do you think I would be doing this?" He gestured around the room.

I wasn't going to let him off the hook this time. "What exactly are you doing, Joe? Who are you? Why did you come here?"

He leaned back on the counter and stretched his long legs out in front of him. "I am just an old man, Ludlow, trying to help those in need."

"But the book, the money. You give all the time. What do you get back?"

"It doesn't have to be about taking. Don't you think it's enough to give? Why should I expect anything in return?"

I was beginning to understand, but it was not easy. I suppose I was still a thief at heart. My whole life in the City had been about taking for myself and taking care of myself.

"You've seen their faces," Joe continued. "You know how they feel when they come at midnight and how they feel when they leave. Why should I want more than that?"

"But they want more," I said.

"And that, Ludlow, is precisely my problem." He turned on his heel and went into the back room. I followed him. He pulled the Black Book out from under the mattress and stood by his bed looking around.

"I've been thinking," he said, "perhaps we should put the book somewhere else."

I couldn't imagine where. The room was hardly big enough for a choice of hiding places.

"Aha," he exclaimed after a few moments. "I have just the place. You can look after it." He swooped down and slid it under my cushion.

I was quite taken aback and struggled not to show it. "Do you think it will be safe?"

"In your hands?" said Joe with a wink. "I'm sure of it. And now, speaking of books, there is a volume I wish to have. Come with me."

And so we went to see Perigoe Leafbinder.

CHAPTER TWENTY-EIGHT

Perigoe Leafbinder

Perigoe Leafbinder had been in the book business for over thirty years, as she liked to remind anyone who came into her shop, and if a book had been printed, she knew about it. Perigoe made a reasonable living but not necessarily from the locals (despite there being little else to do in the dark evenings but read, few had acquired the skill). She operated a very efficient delivery service, by means of a horse and trap, to the north side of the City, where lived the rich and idle, who bought books purely to demonstrate their style and intellectual superiority. Perigoe had learned early that it was not difficult to make money out of other people's vanity.

She was a small woman, almost a dwarf, with a pinched face and a rather crooked smile. In recent months her left eye had developed an irritating twitch, which increased when she was nervous, a state she was in most of the time, with the result that she was constantly winking. Her flared nostrils supported a pair of round spectacles, almost as if

they had been designed for the purpose. They made the arms of her spectacles redundant, for they never fell off even when she bent over. Since her husband's death some three years previously Perigoe had taken to wearing black almost exclusively and, given her size and apparel, was often difficult to see in the dim light. She took great pleasure in emerging from dark corners and tapping browsers on the back, making them jump.

Joe entered the shop, leaving Ludlow outside, and stood for some minutes in the silence surveying his surroundings. He had to stoop somewhat and when he took off his hat his wild hair brushed the oak beams that traversed the ceiling. The walls were shelved and freestanding bookcases stood close together in parallel lines across the floor. Joe walked between them, running his long fingers across the dark spines of the books. There seemed no particular order to the place: Novels sat beside scientific works, art beside mathematics, antiquarian volumes beside new.

Perigoe appeared as if from nowhere and poked him with a wizened forefinger.

"Mr. Zabbidou, I believe." Her voice was almost inaudible. Perigoe always spoke as if she thought someone was eavesdropping.

"Indeed I am," replied Joe. "A pleasure to meet you, Mrs. Leafbinder." He took her bloodless hand in his and kissed it with great ceremony.

Perigoe allowed her hand to linger, remembering for an instant a time when she might have blushed at such a gesture.

"How may I help you?" she asked and winked three times.

"I seek a book," said Joe, "about animals, amphibians in particular, by S. E. Salter. I was hoping that you might possess such a volume."

"Well, I believe I do," said Perigoe and glided across the floor, almost as if she were not in possession of feet, to find it. She returned quickly and handed a book to Joe, a slim volume with a hard cover and color plates. He held it firmly between thumb and forefinger and looked her deep in the eyes. Perigoe found it difficult to avert her gaze.

"I thought you might wish to share a drink with me," he suggested. "Tonight, perhaps?"

Perigoe nodded slowly and her eyelid flapped like a sheet in the wind. She wanted to look away but for some reason she was unable. Soft music filled her head, like early-morning birdsong, and her bony fingertips were beginning to prickle as if she had been stung by nettles.

"At midnight?"

Perigoe nodded again.

"Until then," said Joe, breaking the spell, and he went to the door. He held up the book.

"How much do I owe you?"

Perigoe's heart was fluttering like a trapped moth and she had to steady herself on a shelf. "There's no charge," she whispered.

Joe reached for the doorknob as a dark shadow on the other side filled the frame. He could hear the sound of heavy breathing and moments later Jeremiah Ratchet burst

in like an overfermented bottle of ale popping its cork. When he saw Joe he snorted scornfully. Joe merely stepped back to allow him entrance, tipped his hat in greeting, and slipped out without a backward glance.

As they made their way back to the shop Ludlow wondered what business Jeremiah had with Perigoe. Surely he was not a man of letters. Ludlow tried to read the title of the book Joe now held, something about amphibians, but it was obscured by the folds of his cloak.

To the outsider, compared with most others in the village Perigoe Leafbinder had a good life. She ran a successful business and did not want for money. She had enjoyed her married life, and now she was equally satisfied with widowhood. But still she stood under the three golden orbs at midnight. Like so many of her fellow Pagus Parvians, she harbored a ruinous secret that would not leave her be. She raised her arm in the light of the expectant three-quarter moon.

Joe opened the door before she could knock.

"Mrs. Leafbinder," he said, "I've been expecting you."

Perigoe glided in silently and Joe led her to the back room.

"So what is it you do up here late at night?" she asked and her eyelid twitched rapidly.

"I buy secrets."

Perigoe adjusted her spectacles nervously as she considered what he had just said. Finally she said, "I have a secret I'd like to sell. Will you take it?"

"But of course," replied Joe and handed her a glass. "I am sure that any secret of yours would be of the highest quality and worth a good sum of money."

Perigoe blushed and winked twice, took a small sip of the syrupy liquid, and began.

CHAPTER TWENTY NINE

EXTRACT FROM
THE BLACK BOOK OF SECRETS

The Bookseller's Confession

My name is Perigoe Leafbinder and I have a wretched admission.

The Leafbinders have been in the business of books for nearly two centuries, and I am proud to carry on the tradition. I have spent thirty years of my life in this shop and God willing I should like to spend another thirty, but if I cannot free my tortured mind I doubt I'll see out another year.

There is in existence a book of which three copies are considered immensely valuable. The story itself is not of any great interest or literary worth, merely the simple tale of a mountain shepherd. What makes the book sought after is the fact that the thirteenth line on the thirteenth page is printed backward. No one knows how this happened; some believe the printer was in league with Beelzebub and the words were turned during one of his devilish ceremonies.

Others say the letters were reversed by a flash of lightning from heaven, a sign of approval from the greatest shepherd of them all, the Lord himself. Or maybe it was the printer's young apprentice—he liked a drink and enjoyed a joke. Whatever the reason, out of the two hundred printed copies of the book this mistake occurs only in three.

The whereabouts of two of the three misprinted books is known: One is in a museum in a foreign city, the other is with the family of the shepherd who wrote the tale. They live with their sheep on the mountains and are rarely seen. They have kept it for generations and refuse to sell it at any price. They say that money is of no value to them. The third book had been missing for almost two hundred years. It was thought to no longer exist.

To possess this volume would bring instant fame and wealth and I, like many others, have dreamed for years of finding it, but in vain.

Some months ago I was in my shop when I heard the bell and I saw a frail old woman making her way slowly between the bookcases. She walked stiffly with the aid of two walking sticks. Her left elbow was held tightly against her side, making her slow progress even more painful, and I could see at once that she concealed something beneath her cloak.

I stepped out into her path and greeted her and I led her into the office, where she leaned her sticks against the desk. It was nearly six and I was looking forward to closing up and retiring for the day. In an effort to hurry things along I inquired rather brusquely, "Madam, how may I help you?"

She eyed me with suspicion, and asked, "Do you buy books?"

I nodded.

"What would you say this is worth?"

She took a tatty volume in maroon leather from beneath her cloak and proffered it across the table. She seemed unwilling to let it out of her grasp and I had to tug with some strength to relieve her of it. She kept her little black eyes on me all the time.

I examined the novel, rather carelessly at first, for I felt it could not be of much value. The leather cover was stained and worn, the title was illegible, and it looked as if it had been quite badly treated.

But when I opened it I was quite unprepared for what I saw. There on the title page were the words:

"*The Loneliness of the High Mountain Shepherd* by Arthur Wolman."

My heart lurched in my chest. Could this be the missing third copy? The old lady's eyes were boring into me all the time as I carried out my examination. Casually I turned the pages. They were brown with age and mold and some were stuck together. I reached page thirteen and I was close to apoplexy when I read it. The thirteenth line was reversed.

.yadnuS a no peehs ym raehs ot dekil I

"Hmm," I mused as if of two minds about something. And indeed I was. Imagine, in my hands I held a book that could bring me acclaim and riches, but only then did I realize I could not afford to buy it. In my dreams I had never considered how I would pay for it; I had only ever thought that somehow the book would be mine.

I reasoned that I had two choices. I could pretend the book was worthless and offer the old lady a token amount of money, or I could tell her the truth and then she would go away and sell it to someone who could pay.

The question was: Did she know the value of the book? I could feel droplets of sweat on my forehead and it took all my concentration to stop my hands from shaking. Her eyes were like needles in my skin.

"Well?" she said rather testily.

My answer sealed my miserable fate.

"It is an interesting volume," I said slowly, "but it is not particularly valuable." Those words set me on a path from which there was no return.

She looked disappointed and for one brief instance I allowed myself to hope. Could it be possible she was ignorant of its true worth?

"But," I said, trying to reassure her, "it just so happens that I have a customer who has an interest in this author, so I should be glad to give you ten shillings for it. I am sure you agree that is a generous offer, considering its rather poor condition."

I smiled, charitably, I thought. The old lady smiled back, in a mean-mouthed, tight-lipped sort of way.

Then she opened those thin lips and hissed, "You filthy

liar. You low-down cheat. Do you think I am a fool? That because I walk with sticks I have feathers in my head?"

I had been found out. I stood up and tried to placate her growing fury.

"Perhaps I made a mistake. Let me look again." But it was too late. I was beyond redemption.

"This book is worth many times what you have just offered me and yet you choose to insult me. You are nothing but a crook. Give it back to me."

She reached across the table and snatched at the book and all I could think was that my dream was being taken with it.

"I will take this elsewhere," she said, still tugging. "To someone with integrity."

"I'm sorry," I cried, close to tears. "A moment's weakness. After all, I am only human. I can be tempted." I was still holding on to the book. I couldn't bear to let it go.

"Pshaw," she spat. "I have heard enough."

We struggled across the desktop. First she would hold sway, then I, until finally I gave one mighty wrench and the book came free. The old lady fell backward and I watched in horror as her head cracked on the arm of the chair and she crashed to the floor in a crumpled pile of skin and bone. I ran to her and dropped to my knees at her side, leaning close to see if she was still breathing.

She hissed in my ear, *"yadnuS a no peehs ym raehs ot dekil I,"* and then expired, her final breath fogging my spectacles.

"Oh, Lord above," I muttered. "Now what do I do?" It was

not usual for a customer to die in the shop and I was unsure of the correct procedure. And while I dithered the voice of the Devil, surely it could only be he, piped up in my ear.

"Take the book," he whispered. "Take the book. Who will know?"

I should like to say that I argued, that I engaged in a debate about the immoral nature of his suggestion, but that would be untrue. Instead I picked it up from where I had dropped it and stuffed it behind Gibbon's *Decline and Fall* on a high shelf above the desk. When I turned around I was startled to see Jeremiah Ratchet standing in the open doorway. I had no idea how long he had been there.

"My dear Perigoe," he asked, "what on this miserable earth are you doing?"

"She has died in my shop," I wailed. "She just collapsed."

"So I see," he said.

Dr. Mouldered arrived and Ratchet stood to one side eyeing the scene. His presence made me feel distinctly uncomfortable.

"Heart attack," pronounced Mouldered after the briefest of examinations. Ratchet gave one of his loud snorts and Mouldered closed his bag and hurried away. To my intense relief the undertakers arrived not long after, the body was removed, and Jeremiah left.

That night after dark I came up with a plan. I wanted to sell the book but I had to be careful. I couldn't be sure who else knew the old lady owned it. I had heard of someone in the City who would pay me a good price for such a book and who could be trusted not to reveal my identity. Of course, there would be no celebrity, no fame, but it was a small sacrifice. If I went now, I could be back before dawn and no one would be the wiser. I hid the book in my cloak and stepped outside straight into Jeremiah Ratchet.

"My dear Perigoe," he said in that loathsome way of his, "I wonder what business has you leaving Pagus Parvus at this time of night."

"My own business," I replied sharply. "Now step away and allow me to pass."

He stayed where he was. "I have been thinking over the events of this evening: the death of that poor unfortunate woman, the book . . ."

"The book?"

"There is a price for keeping secrets," he said.

His tone frightened me. "What you are suggesting, Mr. Ratchet?"

"I think that you are on your way to the City to dispose of the book, the very one you stole from the old lady this afternoon, for a rather large sum of money that you will keep all to yourself."

"There is no book, Mr. Ratchet."

"Well," said Jeremiah, "then we have a problem. You see, if you do not find the book, which I know is here, then I will be forced to tell the magistrate that I witnessed that woman's death at your hands. The penalty is hanging, you know, for murder."

"Murder?"

"I saw everything," said Jeremiah. "I watched you attack that old lady and then push her to the ground, only to wrest the book from her dying hand."

"That is not how it happened," I protested, but Jeremiah merely laughed.

"Consider what I have said carefully, Mrs. Leafbinder. I am sure you will come 'round to my way of thinking."

I am ashamed to say that I cursed the duplicitous scoundrel for a full minute, but I knew when I was beaten.

"Tell me what you want, Mr. Ratchet," I said finally.

"It's quite simple, my dear. I wish to have the pick of your shelves whenever I choose and a small payment, shall we say five shillings, on a weekly basis."

"And what of the book?"

He pretended to give the matter some consideration. "Well, I could take it to the City, of course, but I think I shall wait. Perhaps after a few years I will sell it for its full value. Meanwhile, if you would be so kind as to hand it over, I shall keep it safe."

What a heartless, sadistic man stood in front of me. I had no choice but to take his terms. I knew Ratchet would not hesitate to go straight to the magistrate, who I did not doubt could be persuaded with money to believe anything Ratchet wanted, and I would be hanged for murder.

"I'll be back on Friday for my fee," he said and went off with the precious book under his arm.

Needless to state, he has been as good as his word. Every Friday he collects his money and takes whatever else he

pleases. As for *The Loneliness of the High Mountain Shepherd*, I lie in bed every night and curse my greed and stupidity a thousand times. Meanwhile Jeremiah is bringing my business to its knees.

I cannot change what I have done, Mr. Zabbidou, and I am sorry for it. All I want is to sleep again, to forget. ✳

Ludlow put down his quill, laid a sheet of blotting paper between the pages, and closed the book.

Joe took Perigoe's cold hand.

"You will sleep," he said, "now your secret is safe."

"But what of Ratchet?" asked Perigoe, a tremor in her voice. "He still has the book."

"Be patient, Perigoe. He will pay for what he has done. That is all I can say. Now, take this"—he handed her a bag of coins—"and go home to get some rest."

Joe watched as Perigoe walked back to the bookshop. He saw her go in and waited for the lights to go out. Then he went to bed, smiling. Joe Zabbidou had no trouble sleeping.

CHAPTER THIRTY

FRAGMENT FROM
THE MEMOIRS OF LUDLOW FITCH

Perigoe's secret was the last one I wrote in the Black Book. The morning after her visit Joe sent me out for some bread. I greeted the bakers as usual, but their response was icy. Elias served me in silence and his eyes were shooting daggers. The oldest boy, who was behind the counter, couldn't even look at me. I bade them goodbye and left, wondering what I had done to offend them. As I stepped out of the door I saw the other two Sourdough brothers across the street. Usually they liked to walk with me, but today they ran away and watched from farther down the hill. One of them threw a snowball. It hit the side of my head and stung sharply. When I put my hand to the wound it came away bloody and I saw a small stone lying at my feet.

Suddenly the window above me opened and the next second a pail of freezing, dirty water drenched me from head to foot. "That's right," came a jeering voice. "Get back up the hill to your devil friend. We don't want you around here." It was Ruby.

I broke into a run and raced back up to the shop, bursting through the door. I slammed it behind me and threw across the bolt.

"What happened?" asked Joe, noticing the blood on my face.

"I'm not sure," I said, "but Elias wouldn't talk to me and Ruby threw a pail of water on my head."

Joe looked puzzled. "For what reason?"

"I don't know," I spluttered. "All I wanted was a loaf of bread."

I peeled off my cloak and hung it in front of the fire. Joe was sitting, leaning forward with his hands clasped under his chin. I shook my dripping head and drops of water turned to steam on the burning logs.

"Did you know this was going to happen?" I asked. "Is it because of Jeremiah?"

"I don't know about Jeremiah," said Joe slowly, "but I must say I expected something like this."

"Why?"

"Because there is a fine line between gratitude and resentment. Everyone is happy to accept my money—they smile and say thank you, and go away and forget how badly off they were before I arrived. Then they come back looking for more."

I was surprised at the bitterness in his voice. This wasn't the Joe I knew, who harbored no resentment, no ill-feeling,

who took it all in his stride. It unsettled me to see this side to him.

"You sound as if this has happened before," I said.

"It has, but usually I know why."

"Well, whatever the reason, I think it's unfair," I began, but at the same time Saluki suddenly started to croak loudly in the shop and the peace and quiet of the morning was violently interrupted by the sound of a riotous altercation in the street.

Joe leaped up and ran to the door. I followed him, and together we hurried down the hill. The sight that greeted us, were it not for the seriousness of it, would have been quite ridiculous and more suited to the theater. Jeremiah Ratchet and Horatio Cleaver were arguing, actually grappling with each other, in the middle of the road. And the cause of their disagreement? A turkey.

Joe's eyes sparkled. "It has begun," he said.

As we approached the fray it became apparent what was going on.

"You'll not take any more of my meat, you thieving windbag!" shouted Horatio, and the onlookers cheered. It seemed that the whole village had come out to watch: the Sourdoughs, Perigoe, Obadiah, Benjamin Tup, Job Wright, Lily Weaver, Dr. Mouldered, Polly, and even a few faces that were unfamiliar to me.

Ratchet said nothing, just planted his feet more firmly on the ground and pulled with all his might. He held the turkey's legs, Horatio had its head, and the poor dead creature was

near torn in two. Jeremiah was purple with the effort and Horatio's cheeks were a similar shade.

The men were well matched: both stout and solid on the ground. Horatio was slightly taller, but whether this was an advantage or not on the icy road was debatable. The air was filled with cursing and swearing, spit and clouds of breath.

"It's my turkey!" shouted Jeremiah. "You owe me, Horatio."

With one huge tug he managed to unbalance the butcher, who let go of the bird rather than fall over. Jeremiah, of course, fell instead, and to have the turkey was no consolation for his loss of dignity as he spun on the ice three times before coming to a stop at Joe's feet.

The crowd cheered and laughed and clapped as Jeremiah struggled to stand. Only Joe held out his hand to help, but Jeremiah ignored it and took off home, still holding the limp bird.

"Good riddance," shouted Elias Sourdough.

Jeremiah didn't look back. I was surprised. He was not the sort of man to let someone else have the last word.

Horatio came up to Joe in a state of great excitement about what he had just done. I had never thought to see this quiet man so elated.

"Did you see that, Joe?" He was breathing heavily and he was shaking. "I stood up to him. I told him he could take no more of my meat. Just like you said."

He seemed to have forgotten that Jeremiah had the turkey.

He waited for Joe to answer, to pat him on the back, to

congratulate him, but Joe said nothing. His face turned from gray to white and, for an instant only, anger flared in his eyes.

"I didn't say that," he muttered. "I didn't say that at all."

Job Wright, the blacksmith, stepped forward and his mouth was curled in a snarl.

"So," he said, and his voice was brimming with sarcasm, "you've finally come to help us."

"Ratchet's time will come," said Joe simply. "All you have to do is wait. For now, can't you all be happy that your fortunes have changed?"

"But how long must we wait?" asked Obadiah. "You told me Jeremiah would feel the force of your justice."

Horatio looked toward the crowd. "And he told me he'd give him what was coming to him."

Then it was Perigoe's turn. "I've been to him, too," she said as loudly as she could, "and he said he'd make Jeremiah pay."

"That's what he told me," came another voice.

"And me," said someone else. "But I thought I was the only one!"

"What are you talking about?" asked another and his neighbor (who had recently sold his own secret) immediately turned to him and began to tell him all about Joe's midnight confessional and the Black Book.

Suddenly everyone was talking at once as they realized exactly how many of their fellow villagers had secretly visited Joe Zabbidou at the stroke of twelve. Those who had been personally invited to the back room now felt cheated that it wasn't an exclusive service—Joe really did know how to make people feel special—and those who hadn't been invited felt cheated that they had not been considered worthy of the service. Whatever the individual's circumstances, the disgruntled crowd, who only moments ago were laughing at Jeremiah, turned united to Joe Zabbidou and fixed him with an icy glare. I looked at them all, their faces glowing in the cold, their narrow eyes focused on Joe. My palms were damp with cold sweat. These were no longer friendly faces and I was frightened.

Job Wright stood with his legs apart and his powerful arms crossed against his chest. In the absence of any other volunteer, he appeared to have taken on the role of village spokesman.

"So, Mr. Zabbidou, what have you to say to that?"

The chattering stopped instantly. Seconds passed and the silence strained at its seams and threatened to explode. I could see the muscles in Joe's jaw clenching and unclenching and he spoke through gritted teeth.

"I said none of those things. You have twisted my words, words I offered to comfort you."

"Then what exactly did you say?" challenged the blacksmith.

"I said to be patient." Joe looked around the scornful faces before settling on Perigoe and Horatio and Obadiah, who stood together in a nervous huddle. "Is that not the truth?"

At first no one answered.

Then Horatio nodded, shamefaced. "I think maybe you did say that," he said quietly.

Perigoe and Obadiah reddened and nodded, too, but Job wasn't so easily appeased.

"What is this nonsense?" he snorted loudly, slamming his fist into his open palm. "First you promise to help and now, when we ask for that help, you hide behind words. You are no better than Jeremiah Ratchet himself. In fact, you are worse. He at least does what he says."

He turned around and addressed the mesmerized onlookers. Job had them hanging on his every word in a way Stirling Oliphaunt would never have been able. I could hardly believe how he had changed. He, too, had been in at midnight, like the rest of them, and taken the money and peace of mind gladly, but now he seemed intent on leading the village against us.

"Jeremiah Ratchet must be punished for what he has done to us," Job declared. "We've waited long enough. We started without Joe Zabbidou and we'll finish without him."

"Hear! Hear!" said a voice from the back, and a deep rumble of approval rolled through the crowd.

"You don't understand," said Joe, trying to make himself heard above the discontented mutterings. But he was wasting his time. No one was listening to him anymore. All eyes were on Job. Now I was really scared, for me and for Joe. I could feel how angry they were. I wanted to shout at them, to tell them to listen, but no sound came from my mouth.

Job turned to Joe. "You come here," he sneered. "You take our secrets and make false promises. Tell us, what are you going to do with those secrets? How many of us are in your debt?"

"I paid you for your secrets," insisted Joe. "I kept my side of the bargain."

Job pounced. "Aha, so it is about money. And is it not true you paid so much that even if we wanted them back, we couldn't afford them?"

"It was a fair exchange," shouted Joe, by now weary and exasperated. "I never expected the money back." Everyone was talking at once. "You know it is my business."

Job came right up to him until their noses were almost touching.

"Business?" he laughed. "At last we are getting to the truth. Jeremiah Ratchet says he is a businessman. I see you two are no different."

He turned and addressed the restless throng. "Maybe we are going after the wrong man. Maybe Jeremiah Ratchet and our good friend Joe Zabbidou here are in this together!"

I looked at the enraged faces before us and it was hard to believe that these were the same people who had once welcomed Joe with open arms. I could hear the words *liar* and *cheat* and I was incensed. I took a step forward, thinking I might be able to protect him, but Joe held me back.

"It is not like that," he said. "I have told you no lies. I never promis—"

But Joe couldn't finish because the crowd had turned against him. They began to boo and hiss.

Joe stood there in a daze, his arms hanging loosely by his sides. People began to pelt him with snow and gravel and anything they could find. I grabbed his hand and dragged him

away. I knew we were in danger out here in the open. I looked back only once and to my dismay I saw Jeremiah Ratchet standing on his doorstep. His arms were folded across his chest and when he caught my eye he opened his mouth and began to laugh.

I locked up the shop and pulled down the blinds. We stayed inside for the rest of the day. I couldn't believe what had happened and I paced between the rooms, going over and over it in my head.

"How could they do this to you? After everything you've done for them."

Joe sat calmly by the fire. He heard my rantings but didn't reply. He hardly said a word the entire afternoon, but I could tell that his mind was working furiously. What was he planning? Revenge on the village or revenge on Jeremiah? Surely it had to be one or the other. In my heart, though, I knew it was neither. Revenge was not Joe's way.

Joe seemed to be talking to himself, reassuring himself that he had done nothing wrong. "I have always paid a fair price," he muttered. "When the deal is done, it is done and no one owes anyone. But still for these people it's not enough. They accused me of making false promises."

"They misunderstood you," I said.

He looked up at me. "I promised nothing. Jeremiah has no hold over me, but that doesn't mean I can do anything

about him." His face was screwed into a deep frown and his eyebrows were almost touching. "There are rules and I must obey them."

"Rules? What rules?" I asked. But Joe was talking to himself again.

"I gave them money, far more than they deserved, and I told them to be patient. That is all. It is hardly a commitment. But now they treat me as if I have betrayed them. Why must it be in human nature to hear one thing but to believe that it is another?"

"Because we want things to get better," I said. "Otherwise, we would all give up."

Joe closed his eyes. "*Dum spiro, spero,*" he said. "While I breathe, I hope."

CHAPTER THIRTY-ONE

The Reluctant Messenger

Down at the Pickled Trout Benjamin Tup was struggling to cope with his customers' demands. He had never had to deal with a full tavern before and tonight the place was heaving with the villagers, some of whom, such as Perigoe Leafbinder, had never even been over the threshold. They sat and stood and leaned and perched on every available surface in a tight circle, somehow managing at the same time to hold on to a mug or a jug of ale. Job Wright was the only one who was reasonably comfortable, having taken center stage on a rickety, ale-stained table.

"Fellow villagers," he boomed to the excited and slightly tipsy crowd, "I say the time has come to take back what is rightfully ours. You all saw Horatio this afternoon, a braver man I have never seen. The way he held on to that turkey is something I will not forget for the rest of my years."

Horatio blushed at the praise and staggered under the

slapping hands that rained down on his back. He covered his ears as deafening cheers rattled his brain.

"But this is only the beginning," continued Job. "All this time we thought it was Jeremiah who was the source of our misfortune. But now we know, he is merely the lackey of Joe Zabbidou. Stirling was right, Joe is the Devil and he is playing his evil games with us. Is there any one of us here who can say we are not in his debt?"

"We all owe him," they shouted back. "Each and every one of us."

"He had us fooled," said Job grimly. "But it's not too late. We can still stop him."

Only one voice dissented and that belonged to Polly. She jumped up on the table and stood in front of Job. The villagers were surprised into an uneasy silence.

"Don't listen to this," she urged. "It's not Joe we have to worry about. It's Jeremiah. Joe helped you all. Why are you doing this to him?"

Some of the villagers, the more sober among them, murmured that Polly had a point.

"The girl's right," said Lily Weaver. "Shouldn't we deal with Jeremiah first?"

Elias Sourdough then climbed up onto the table, which now shook alarmingly. "No," he said. "It's Joe needs sorting. And if you want proof, listen to this." He reached into his pocket and took out a piece of paper and read from it.

"If you wont to keepe yore seecret leve five shilins at the churche gattes tonite and I'll say nuffin."

The crowd gasped.

"Yes," said Elias, "a blackmail letter, left secretly in my shop, no doubt by Ludlow, and written by none other than Joe Zabbidou. And this is only the beginning. Who will be blackmailed next?"

The villagers needed no more convincing, and outside the tavern, hidden in the shadows, with his ear pressed up against the window, Jeremiah Ratchet also heard what Elias had to say. As he listened an ugly, wet-lipped smirk spread across his fleshy cheeks. Now he knew everything.

Polly's heart sank. *I've got to tell Ludlow,* she thought, creeping out of the tavern and darting away up the hill. She rapped loudly on the pawnbroker's door until Ludlow finally let her in and brought her through to the back room. Polly stood uncomfortably in front of the fire, twitching and wringing her hands. Her face was pale and she licked her lips nervously.

"What can I do for you, my dear?" asked Joe evenly.

"There's something I've got to tell you." Her voice was barely above a whisper. "Something I think you should know."

In the corner Ludlow paled. What could she mean? *Don't tell him what we did,* he urged her silently.

"I want to help you." She was almost apologetic, and then the words tumbled out all over each other. "I'm here to warn you. I think you are in danger. Since the turkey fight everyone's been in the Pickled Trout. They're all so angry. I've heard some awful threats. Something dreadful is going to happen, I just know it."

"To me or to Ratchet?" murmured Joe.

The answer was clear in Polly's eyes. "Now that everyone knows what you do at midnight, they're all talking about the Black Book. They think you used magic to charm their secrets out of them."

"Magic?" Joe raised his eyebrows in mild surprise.

"Obadiah said you gave him an enchanted potion to loosen his tongue."

Joe's eyes widened. "What pyretic brains these people have. It's nothing more than brandy, to calm their nerves."

"Job says you paid all that money so they'd always be in your debt. He says you're trying to take over from Jeremiah Ratchet."

"He's just a troublemaker," tutted Joe dismissively. "So the villagers have taken a dislike to me because I paid them too much? This is madness."

"They judge you by the standards they know, and all they know is Jeremiah Ratchet. You promised things—"

"No," he interrupted sharply. He never promised.

Polly corrected herself. "They *believe* you promised them help but now you've fallen back on your word, like Ratchet." She paused for a second. "And then there was the letter."

"Letter?" Joe and Ludlow spoke in unison.

Polly shifted uncomfortably. "I didn't believe it until Elias Sourdough showed it to everyone in the tavern. He read it out. It's a blackmail letter. He says it's from you. It says you want five shillings at the church gates tonight to keep quiet about his secret."

"So that's why they wouldn't talk to me," exclaimed Ludlow.

"They think I wrote a blackmail letter? For five shillings?" Joe laughed in utter amazement. "They believe I have started to threaten them?"

"Yes," said Polly hurriedly. "And if you want to win back their trust then you have to show that you're on their side. Before they do something terrible."

"Whose side do they think I am on?"

She didn't answer, just nodded down the hill.

"Tell me," said Joe in a voice that was strangely flat, "how do I prove otherwise? What would they have me do with Jeremiah?"

"Maybe you could give the potion—I mean brandy—to Jeremiah."

"And if I do? What then?"

Polly looked a little embarrassed. "Under the influence of the brandy, he is bound to admit to a terrible crime and then you can blackmail him back."

I snorted loudly. Joe would never do something as underhanded as that.

"This is beyond belief!" thundered Joe. "Blackmail is not my business."

"I'm sorry, Mr. Zabbidou," said Polly quickly, shrinking back against the fireplace. "I'm only trying to help. Everyone's so angry with you. I just thought you should know."

"What of Jeremiah?" asked Joe suddenly. "What does he know of this?"

Polly shook her head. "I don't know. Maybe nothing. But

I'm sure he's up to something, too. He had one of the Sour-dough boys in his study the other day. I just wish I knew why."

Joe shook his head wearily and leaned against the mantel. "How it saddens me to see how quickly men turn against each other."

Polly looked desperately at Ludlow. "Please be careful," she said and then she was gone.

CHAPTER THIRTY-TWO

FRAGMENT FROM
THE MEMOIRS OF LUDLOW FITCH

After Polly left Joe took out the brandy and two glasses and set them on the mantel. Then he sat down heavily and closed his eyes. "Now we must wait," he said.

"Are you expecting someone?"

"Perhaps."

"Should I fetch the book?"

"Not yet."

I sat at the table. What else could I do? I was trembling, I had been all day, and my mouth was dry. I heard the church bell ring every hour. Midnight came and went, and all outside was still. My lids became heavy and I rested my head on the table and began to doze and then to dream. I was running for my life. I knew there was someone behind me but I couldn't see who it was. Every time I looked back I was blinded by a glinting light that came out of the darkness. My lungs were screaming and my legs were leaden. I tried to call out but I couldn't open my mouth. Pa emerged from the mist again and threw me to the ground and started to choke me. I could hear Ma and someone else running toward us, their footsteps pounding like hammers.

I woke, shaking and with my heart racing, but the hammering continued. Someone was banging on the door. Joe was already in the shop. I knew who it was. There was only one man in Pagus Parvus who would feel the need to make his presence known in such a heavy-handed fashion.

Jeremiah Ratchet.

I ran through and saw Jeremiah's huge silhouette blocking out the light from the moon. His fist was raised ready to come down again, but Joe was already there and opened the door so quickly that Jeremiah fell in.

"Hurrumph," he snorted, predictably, as he steadied himself.

"Ah, Mr. Ratchet, what a pleasant surprise."

Jeremiah planted his feet firmly on the shop floor and took a good look around as if he was claiming the territory for his own. He saw the frog and for a second the two creatures eyed each other with interest, though Saluki's waned first. Then he pushed his way past and went into the back room. Joe went after him. I slipped in and sat at the table and shrank against the wall, trying to hide in the shadows.

Jeremiah stood at the fire warming the seat of his pants. He folded his arms and wrinkled his nose, as if the place had a bad smell. Joe poured a couple of brandies, large and small, and handed the large one to his visitor. Jeremiah drank it in a single gulp.

"Mr. Zabbidou," he said, "I'll come straight to the point. I am not the type to mince words. I believe in saying what's what."

"And that is?" Joe was strangely calm, but my stomach was turning over and over.

"You had me foxed for a while, but I've worked it out now. I know your game."

He waited for Joe to respond, a smug smile across his cheeks as if he expected praise.

"My game?"

"I'll not deny it, you've caused me and my business no end of trouble. At first I thought you were plotting against me. I've seen the comings and goings in the middle of the night. The villagers thought you were some sort of hero, but I couldn't understand why. To me you were just a nuisance. But now I know what you do and I'm here because I want you to help me."

He seemed nervous and droplets of sweat oozed from his hairline. He dabbed at them with his handkerchief.

"What?" I exclaimed before I could stop myself. I looked at Joe. "You don't believe this, do you?"

Joe signaled to me to be quiet. "How can I help, Mr. Ratchet?"

Jeremiah sighed deeply and sat down heavily, wedging his quivering posterior into the armchair. Then to my astonishment he began to sob. It was not a pleasant sight.

"I wish to unburden myself of a terrible secret," he mumbled through his tears. "I didn't know whom else to turn to. You are the only one who can help."

I could hardly contain myself. Ratchet wanting to confess? Ratchet sobbing? This had to be some sort of trick. But Joe carried on as if this behavior were completely normal.

"And how can I do that?" asked Joe kindly.

Jeremiah looked out through his chubby fingers. "With the book," he said. "The Black Book of Secrets."

I shook my head in disgust. Jeremiah Ratchet did not deserve even a drop of ink in that book. I was about to say as much, but Joe spoke before me.

"A wise decision," he said. "Ludlow, fetch the book, please."

I was paralyzed with confusion. Joe was going along with this charade. He was going to buy Ratchet's secret. Why? To blackmail him, like Polly said? Surely Joe would never do anything like that!

"The book, Ludlow," repeated Joe pointedly.

With dragging feet I went to fetch it, aware of Ratchet's eyes on me all the time. I pulled the book out from under my cushion and was about to lay it on the table when, with a loud sucking noise, Jeremiah launched himself from his chair and came right at me. The speed of his approach was surprising, his bulk gave him great momentum, and I put up my hands to shield myself. Jeremiah threw himself against me and with a violent shove sent me crashing into the table. Out of the corner of my eye I saw the book spin

off toward the ceiling, its pages flapping and turning, and then a huge swollen hand reached up and snatched it from midair.

Jeremiah Ratchet was in possession of the Black Book of Secrets.

CHAPTER THIRTY-THREE

There ensued a rather comical scene. Jeremiah had the advan-
tages of surprise and weight, but these were countered by
the brandy he had consumed. Joe was light on his feet and
was the faster of the two. With speed that defied the laws of
physics, Joe leaped over the back of his chair, displaying the
grace and agility of a young gazelle. In two strides he was at
Jeremiah's side and he whipped the book from his sweaty
clutches. Jeremiah cursed and lurched like a drunken elephant from one side of the room to the other, while Joe
merely sidestepped his clumsy attempts to grab it back. I
watched uselessly from the floor where I had fallen, severely
winded, after sustaining the impact of Jeremiah's full weight.

The entire display lasted no longer than a minute. Jeremiah was forced to give up and slid down the wall to sit in a
most undignified fashion with his legs splayed and his mouth
wide open. His face was bright red, his eyes were bulging,
and his lungs rattled with every drawn breath.

Joe stood over him, his clothes disheveled and his hair wilder than ever. His spidery shadow danced gleefully on the wall. I dragged myself up and joined him.

"I must protest at your behavior, Mr. Ratchet," scolded Joe. "It is not what I would expect from a man of your standing."

Jeremiah struggled to his feet.

"Listen, Mr. Zabbidou," he said and all pretense of sobbing and remorse was gone. "You don't seem to understand. You're finished in this place. The villagers are coming to get you. You'll be run out of here. But before you go, I want the book. And what I want I get."

I laughed. Poor Ratchet. He was the one who didn't understand. Joe would never give up the book.

"Absolutely not," said Joe. "The book is confidential and I will never surrender it."

"Ah now, Zabbidou," persisted Jeremiah, and Joe winced with distaste at this familiarity, "don't be like that. What use is the book to you anymore? Why take it with you when I can have it and make good use of it? We're both businessmen, Zabbidou. To keep it would be nothing short of spiteful."

"Exactly what would you do with it, Mr. Ratchet?" asked Joe.

Jeremiah looked surprised. "Blackmail, of course. Only I'd make a better job of it than you. Five shillings at the church gate? Not very sophisticated, if you don't mind my saying."

I stood openmouthed at the sheer cheek of the man.

"Joe didn't write that letter," I began, but Joe motioned with his hand for me to be quiet.

"Under the circumstances, Mr. Ratchet," he said, "I do not feel I can take your pledge. I think it is time for you to go."

Jeremiah surprised us both and held up his hands in surrender. "As you wish," he said and made his way meekly into the shop. I watched from the doorway as Jeremiah stopped at Saluki's tank and placed his hands on the lid. Now what was he going to do?

"Give me the book," he hissed at Joe through his yellow teeth, "or I will kill your precious frog."

"I'm warning you," said Joe quietly. "Do not touch the frog. She does not like it."

" 'She does not like it,' " mimicked Jeremiah like a petulant child. "Give me the book and it won't matter."

"Don't touch the frog." Joe's voice was menacing.

"Ha!" shouted Jeremiah and he flung the lid away, reached in, and grabbed Saluki with both hands.

"No!" shouted Joe, but it was too late.

Jeremiah yelped and dropped her. Saluki landed on the floor with a soft thud and sat very still, looking a little dazed.

"I think it bit me," Jeremiah said, his eyes wide with surprise and confusion. "I think it bit me." Undeterred and desperate, he picked up the tank and raised it above his head.

"Give me the damned book or the frog gets it."

Joe, and Saluki, looked at him sadly. "Believe me," said Joe, stepping into the shop, "it won't do you any good." And

at that he handed the Black Book of Secrets to Jeremiah Ratchet.

Jeremiah's eyes shone as he snatched the book with a triumphant crow. "I'll be the judge of that."

Without another word he stomped out and slammed the door. Gracefully and precisely, Saluki climbed up the counter and back into her tank. Joe replaced the lid and dropped in a couple of bugs and the frog chewed them as if nothing had happened. And it was strange, I never thought a frog could look satisfied, but at that moment I swear Saluki did. Her colors glowed with a vibrancy that near lit up the room and her bright eyes seemed to say, "You were warned, Ratchet. You were warned."

CHAPTER THIRTY-FOUR

Departure

J eremiah Ratchet was gripped by intense glee. He longed to skip, but the icy road permitted only a short-stepped, cautious haste. So instead he punched the air with his fist and let out an audible "Ha! Ha!" into the night.

He was distinctly pleased with himself. He had guessed quite rightly that the Black Book was the key. To possess it now almost made up for his earlier humiliation at the hands of Horatio and the turkey. And, of course, if it hadn't been for that altercation, he would never have found out exactly what was in the book. After he had gone home with the turkey he had watched the crowd, and Joe and Ludlow, from his window. He had heard it all, every single word. What fools they were, those villagers, to trust their secrets to Joe Zabbidou. And that was when he had come up with his plan, to pretend to wish to pawn his own secret so he could get his hands on the book. When he eavesdropped outside the Pickled Trout, that had been just the icing on the cake.

How stupid Joe had been to send the blackmail letter. He had burned all of his bridges in the village and at the same time he had done Jeremiah a great favor. By the time the villagers had gotten rid of Joe it would be too late. Jeremiah would have the Black Book and he would use it to regain his rightful position of power in Pagus Parvus.

If he was honest with himself, in his heart of hearts Jeremiah had never thought it would be so easy to take possession of the Black Book of Secrets. But then who would have thought Joe would surrender it rather than lose his precious frog? Jeremiah was fit to burst with self-congratulation.

As quietly as this delight would allow he hurried inside, unaware that he had omitted to shut the door fully. He was also unaware of the small figure that crept in after him and followed him to the study. This stealthy intruder curled up in the darkest corner and watched and waited. The full moon shone its dusty beams through the window. They lit up the clock on the mantel to show a quarter after three. Jeremiah threw off his coat and dropped it; he pulled off his hat and tossed it aside. With every step he took snow fell off his boots and melted on the rug, leaving dark stains. He held up the prize in triumph, the red ribbon trailing from between its pages.

"I'll show them," he laughed, waving it in the air. "They'll all pay for their treachery."

Jeremiah took himself over to the dying fire and eased himself into one of his very expensive leather chairs. He glanced at the cover of the book, but couldn't understand it, so he flung it open and laid it flat on his lap. He licked the tip of his stubby forefinger and turned the pages with obvious relish, slowly at first and then more quickly. He tittered, he giggled, he took the Lord's name in vain more than once, stopping every so often to rub his hands together. He did this not in glee, however, but to soothe his burning palms. Saluki's bite, if that is what she had done, was proving to be nearly as irritating as her owner.

"My fortune is made," gloated Jeremiah. "There're secrets in this book I couldn't even have guessed. And not just from Pagus Parvus, from all over. As for Dr. Mouldered! My, my, who'd have thought it!"

With great satisfaction he snapped the book shut and a single page fluttered to the floor to land at his feet. Breathing hard by now, he leaned forward to retrieve it and held it up to the light. Its ragged edge suggested that it had been recently torn from another book. It showed a colorful picture, hand-painted with some skill.

"Frogs?" snorted Jeremiah disdainfully and glanced curiously at the caption. Seconds later he fell back into the chair and let out a tremendous groan.

"What has he done?" he moaned. "The lanky fork-tongued devil, he has duped me."

His hands throbbed and burned. His movements were slowing. A creeping numbness spread up his arms and throughout his body. His chest tightened, his throat swelled.

It was becoming difficult to breathe. But he watched, unable even to express surprise, as the boy emerged from the half-light and came forward.

"Who's there?" Jeremiah stuttered hoarsely.

The boy didn't answer, just stared at the dying man before bending down to pick up the book from the floor.

"Who has done this to you?" whispered the intruder.

Jeremiah's lips moved and silently formed a single word.

The boy shook his head and left.

CHAPTER THIRTY FIVE

FRAGMENT FROM
THE MEMOIRS OF LUDLOW FITCH

As soon as Jeremiah was gone, I turned on Joe. Even now I still couldn't piece the puzzle together. All I knew was that he had let Jeremiah walk away with his most precious possession.

No, I thought, *my most precious possession, too.*

That book was now part of my very existence. I couldn't stop myself, and blinded by rage and disappointment, I beat upon Joe's chest with my fists.

"Why did you let him take it? You know how he will use it."

Joe shook me off gently and infuriated me with a smile. "Calm down, Ludlow. Don't you understand? This is what we've been waiting for."

He poured another brandy (I had never seen him drink more than one), threw back his head, and swallowed it in one go.

"I have to say the fellow had me worried somewhat. I thought he would have been up here days ago; it would

have saved us a lot of trouble. He has certainly taken his time."

Confused, angry, and burning with questions, I was determined to find the truth.

"You mean you wanted him to do this?"

"It's not what I want," said Joe, "it's what Jeremiah wants. If nothing else he was true to his nature. That man cannot bear others to have what he desires."

"You're talking in riddles again. Just tell me what's really going on. I deserve to know."

"What do you want to know, Ludlow? What is it you think I have kept from you?"

His calm disarmed me. My anger dissipated and I became flustered. "Lots of things. You said you weren't a blackmailer yet you asked Jeremiah for a secret, just like Polly said. Would you have paid him, too?"

Joe looked mildly shocked. "I expected better of you than such an accusation. Jeremiah, for all his faults, deserves a chance, like everyone else, to gain relief from his troubles. Do you think that his innate cruelty prevents him from feeling remorse? I had to give him the opportunity. It is part of what I do."

"The opportunity to do what?"

"To say he was sorry."

"And if he had, what then?"

"Well, if he had told me a secret, then I should have paid him. Rules are rules. Things would have been different, of course; as it is, he has only himself to blame."

I tutted with exasperation. "And just what are these rules you live by?"

He remained silent.

"Who are you, Joe?"

"The truth will come later, I promise you that," he said finally. "What is important now is that you go to retrieve the book."

I laughed sarcastically. "And how am I to do that?"

"You'll find a way, but you'd better hurry. He must be halfway down the hill already."

"You're not coming with me?"

Joe shook his head. "I have played my part. Now it is your turn."

I threw up my hands in frustration, but I didn't waste another second. Whatever else I wanted to say to Joe, it could wait. He was right. I had to get the Black Book back. The secrets of the whole village, and others, were in there. Jeremiah already knew Perigoe's and Horatio's and Obadiah's, but what about everyone else's? There were so many secrets. I realized that until now I had thought of this whole business as a sort of game that Joe and I were playing with the villagers, all of us pitted against Jeremiah Ratchet. But it wasn't a game any longer. It was deadly serious. I had written their confessions and now it was up to me to save them.

So I ran out of the door and down the hill, skidding and slipping and cursing in my head both Jeremiah and Joe, and plagued by terrible doubt. Maybe Job Wright hadn't been so

far off the mark. Maybe Joe was using the villagers and I had been too blind to see it, selfishly hanging on to this new life, so desperate for a real father that I had ignored what was going on under my nose. Was this the punishment for taking what I didn't deserve? But it still didn't make sense.

"It's not about the money," I said to the night. "There has to be another reason."

Jeremiah had already gone inside, but in his haste the latch hadn't caught, so I slipped into the hall and followed his trail of wet footprints to the study. I squatted down just inside the door and watched as he settled in the chair. There was meat pie somewhere close by and the smell made my mouth water.

I didn't know what I was going to do. My heart beat so loudly I thought it would give me away. I could see the top of his head and I could hear pages turning. Soon it would be too late, he would know everything. I heard the book snap shut and saw a page flutter to the floor. He leaned forward to pick it up. He said something, then groaned and fell back into the chair. All I could hear now was his noisy wheezing.

I don't know how long I waited before tiptoeing over. He was so still I wondered if he had fallen asleep. I stood right in front of him. His eyes were open and for a second I expected him to grab me, but he just sat there, a terrible sight to behold. His face was white and his breathing was harsh and rattling. I knew I was looking at a dying man.

"Who's there?" he mumbled and I could hardly hear him.

I bent down and picked up the book from the floor.

"Who has done this to you?" I asked.

Slowly Jeremiah's dry lips formed a silent word.

Joe.

There was nothing else I could do, so I left.

CHAPTER THIRTY-SIX

Fragment from
The Memoirs of Ludlow Fitch

Jeremiah's dying word had shattered my world. When I looked into his eyes I could see no lie. I walked slowly back up the hill and my heart was leaden. I was torn up inside. All this time I had thought Joe was better than the rest of us, better than I could ever hope to be, but in the end he was as bad as my own ma and pa, if not worse; to my knowledge they at least had never willfully killed anyone. Yes, like everyone else, I had wanted Joe to stand up to Jeremiah Ratchet. But I had never thought it would end like this. There was no other way to say it. Joe Zabbidou was a murderer.

But how did he do it?

I went over and over in my head the last meeting between the two of them, searching for clues. There was no weapon and Jeremiah wasn't injured in any way. Perhaps he was poisoned. But how was it administered? It could have been the brandy. But both had drunk from the same bottle. Then maybe it was in the glass.

That was it! Joe had put poison in Jeremiah's glass before pouring the brandy. Jeremiah had drunk it in one gulp and then, presumably to Joe's delight, he had washed it down with more.

Joe was waiting for me by the fire, a glass in his hand, and he looked as if nothing out of the ordinary had happened. He had even straightened out the room.

"Did you get it?"

I handed it over.

"Good work. I knew I could trust you."

I wanted to say something, but I was still too shocked to speak. Then I noticed his satchel on the table. It was buckled and bursting at the seams. A small drawstring bag sat beside it. Icy fear ran in my veins. I found my voice.

"You're not going, are you?"

He put up his hand to silence me.

"Shh," he said. "Listen."

Something was happening outside. I could hear the murmur of voices and the sound of feet breaking through the frozen snow. I crept to the door and looked into the shop. Cloaked shapes moved on the other side of the window with faces like devils lit up in the light of flaming torches. And among them I could see the stooped outline of Obadiah Strang and beside him the tiny figure of Perigoe Leafbinder and beside her the thickness of Horatio Cleaver.

"Come out, Joe Zabbidou," chanted the shadows, a hundred strong, "or we'll burn you out."

At the sight of this demonic throng my legs went weak and I staggered back to Joe in terror. "They're out there, all of them," I hissed. "They've come for us, like Polly said. They're going to kill us."

But Joe stayed where he was and took a long, slow draught of his drink.

"Just be patient," he said. "Just be patient."

"There's no time for patience," I snapped in a panic, clutching at his cloak.

He took me by the wrists and held me away from him. "Not yet."

"Come out, Joe Zabbidou, come out!" The voices swelled into a menacing chorus. Then with a tremendous crash the shopfront window shattered and the counter was sprayed with splintered glass and the room was filled with smoke and the smell of burning oil and the sharp crackle of flames. Outside on the street they were kicking at the door and beating it down with cudgels. The noise was deafening, the smoke black and choking, the heat intensifying.

"Come out, Joe Zabbidou," they cried. "Come out!"

Still he wouldn't move and he wouldn't let go. I tried to pull away, but his grip was like a vice. "Are you going to let me die, too?" I shouted, but he didn't hear me. His head was cocked to one side and he was listening intently.

I began to scream and yell. The abominable cacophony outside rose to an inhuman pitch. Clouds of smoke rolled

into the back room until I could barely see my own hand in front of my face. At last, out of all this madness there came another voice. A shrill voice that carried above the confusion. Polly's voice.

"Ratchet's dead! Jeremiah Ratchet's dead."

Joe released my wrists and raised his arms in triumph above his head.

"*Acta est fabula,*" he said. "It is over."

CHAPTER THIRTY-SEVEN

Leftovers

Polly had woken in the night but she didn't know why. Now that she was awake, she felt hungry. Certain that Jeremiah would be in bed, she took a candle and crept down the stairs. On her way to the kitchen she noticed that the front door was open and she closed it. So he had gone out after all. "I suppose he'll be back soon enough, drunk as a lord," she muttered. Then she saw the light in the study and went in.

The dinner tray from the previous evening was on the desk, and Polly shook her head in irritation. She hated to see good food go to waste. A slice of pie sat on the plate, untouched. She nibbled at a piece of crust and immediately spat out what she took to be a bit of grit and wrinkled her nose.

"That's one of Horatio Cleaver's pies," she said to herself. The butcher had brought it to the house personally only that evening. She made a mental note to tell Horatio what she thought of it next time she saw him. Then she noticed

damp footprints on the rug that led to the fire, the hat and scarf tossed on the floor.

"Lord above," she exclaimed, hastily wiping any telltale crumbs from her mouth. "Mr. Ratchet, what are you doing here?"

Polly could see the top of his head—instantly identifiable by the shiny bald patch in the middle—above the back of the chair and his remaining hair, gray and white in color, sticking out defiantly over his ears despite daily applications of expensive hair lotion. She rounded the chair cautiously to meet Jeremiah's open-eyed stony gaze of death and screamed.

Nobody would ever claim that Jeremiah Ratchet was an attractive man. He had all the appearance of a toad about to burst. In death he was little changed, just less flexible, sitting stiffly in the chair. In his hand he still had the loose page, held fast between his rigid fingers. Polly wasn't interested in what he had been reading (though she was struck by the beauty of the picture), but she was mesmerized by the expression on his face. His mouth was fixed open in a sort of grimacing yawn and his eyes were unnaturally wide. It was as if he had just been told something truly shocking.

Poor Polly had never encountered a corpse at such close quarters, and it took some moments for her to gather her wits. Once gathered, however, she proved to be a practical girl. With trembling fingers she reached into Jeremiah's waistcoat and found his purse, which she stuffed down the front of her apron. For a moment she beheld poor Jeremiah for the last time. Then she stepped back and hit her foot

against something hard behind her. She looked down to see the coal scuttle.

"Only the flames of hell will warm your cold soul," she mumbled before running out to the street and announcing to the village in her shrill voice:

"Ratchet's dead! Jeremiah Ratchet's dead."

CHAPTER THIRTY-EIGHT

Diagnosis

During his lifetime Jeremiah had successfully kept the villagers at bay; within minutes of his death, however, his house was swarming with them. They ran up and down the stairs, opening and closing doors and pocketing what they could conceal beneath their coats. For one reason or another they all felt they deserved something.

"I heard that his bathtub was pure gold," whispered one as he crammed a polished spittoon into his breast pocket.

"And that he ate only from silver platters and drank from the finest crystal," said his companion, wrenching a fine brass sconce from the wall.

A third man was very busy tapping the stair panels with his hairy knuckles. He was looking for secret passages that led to underground cellars where jewelry and treasure and, more important, ale and wine were said to be stored.

"'Ere 'e is," came the youngest Sourdough's cry from below. "Oooh, 'e's gorn black and blue."

With a great rushing noise the crowd arrived at the study and poured in to gather around Ratchet's chair like water meeting a rock in a stream. It was quite true; Jeremiah's skin had taken on a rather strange mottled hue. This, combined with the yellowish foam at the corners of his mouth and his repulsive grimace, was too much for Lily Weaver. With a deep sigh she swooned and would have fallen to the floor except the crush was so great she remained standing, and came to some moments later supported on all sides by her fellow Pagus Parvians. Then she was lifted up and passed over the sea of heads, as a bottle taken by the tide, only to be dropped unceremoniously into the corridor.

A voice cried out above the hubbub and, with much pushing and shoving and elbowing, Dr. Samuel Mouldered managed to enter the room.

"Thank the 'eavens above yore 'ere," said Elias Sourdough. "Ratchet's kicked the bucket at last."

The room quietened in anticipation of Mouldered's assessment of the case. Few of the villagers were acquainted with the fad of self-diagnosis (with the aid of Dr. Moriarti's *Simplified Medical Dictionary for the Common Man*, available at a small discount from Perigoe Leafbinder's bookshop). They preferred to hear it from the horse's mouth.

Mouldered walked around the chair several times, stroking his sparsely whiskered chin. It was not often he got to hold center stage in this way, and his nerves, tightly wound these past few days, were getting the better of him. Sweat squeezed

out of the furrows of his brow and he licked his dry lips with a pale pink tongue. Finally he cleared his throat and announced hoarsely, "I believe that Jeremiah Ratchet has suffered some sort of fit, or apoplexy, of the heart which has caused his untimely death."

The crowd sighed and an air of disappointment was quite apparent. They had been expecting foul play. Certainly it would not have been undeserved.

"'E looks sort of smothered to me. And 'is 'ands don't look right. Are you sure?"

That Jeremiah might have been smothered was little more than wishful thinking but, upon closer inspection, Mouldered could not deny that his palms were quite red and blistered, as if they had been severely burned.

"I'm sure," he said, with all the conviction of a man who isn't. "Sometimes heart attacks make people's hands, er—" he fumbled in his pockets as if searching for the correct medical term but gave up and finished lamely—"look like this."

Eyebrows were raised, sniggers were barely suppressed, and heads were shaken, but Mouldered refused to say any more and, the excitement over, the villagers shuffled out, jingling and jangling with their hidden spoils. In the silence they left behind them Mouldered closed Jeremiah's eyes with quivering fingers. He took the sheet of paper from his hand, glanced at it briefly, then folded it and was about to pocket it when Perigoe appeared.

"That belongs to Joe," she said. "It's from a book of mine he bought about amphibians."

"Ah, Perigoe," said Mouldered, handing it to her, "then perhaps you could see to it that he gets it."

She nodded and left quickly, clutching a single tatty maroon book under her arm.

Just one? thought Mouldered. *How very restrained.*

CHAPTER THIRTY-NINE

Fragment from
The Memoirs of Ludlow Fitch

As soon as the crowd heard that Ratchet was dead they had turned tail, one and all, and ran down the hill. Joe went straight through to the shop and began to beat out the flames with an old coat from the window. To be honest, it was more smoke than fire and it didn't take long to put it out. Despite that, the damage was extensive. Everything was charred or blackened with smoke and the acrid smell made breathing quite unpleasant. There was little worth saving. Gradually the air was clearing due to the biting wind that now blew through the broken window and the shattered door. I helped him without knowing why. Eventually Joe stamped out one last stubborn flame and rested, panting from the effort.

"What a dreadful shame, so unnecessary," he murmured. "But I suppose it could have been worse. At least I still have this." He bent down and pulled the wooden leg, miraculously unharmed, from the rubble and went to the back

room. When I looked in he was dressed in cloak and scarf and struggling to force the leg into the satchel.

Suddenly everything was happening far too quickly. I was angry with Joe for the way he behaved, for the murder I was so sure he had committed, but I was frightened, too, because he was leaving.

"Is that it? You're just going to go?"

"There's not much more I can do now," he said. "I have no reason to stay."

"What about the shop?"

"The shop is finished. We can start again somewhere else." He slung the bag over his shoulder and came through, stepping carefully over the wreckage on his way to the door. "You are coming with me?"

How could he be so calm? My heart was racing.

I hesitated. "I don't know if I can."

"Oh." He sounded as if he hadn't considered this and frowned. "I thought you knew we couldn't stay here forever. Perhaps I should have said something before. My work compels me to move on."

"It's not that," I said. "I would have gone anywhere with you but—" I couldn't say it. I felt as if I was choking. We faced each other wordlessly until the silence was gently broken by a soft voice that made us both look up. It was Perigoe.

"Mr. Zabbidou," she said. "Mr. Zabbidou." She came through the remains of the door, and when she saw the destruction she looked distraught. "I want to say sorry," she

whispered. "Everyone wants to say sorry. We know we were wrong to treat you the way we did. We should have trusted you. It was the letter that frightened us all."

"Ah," said Joe, "the letter."

Perigoe looked as if she was about to burst into tears. "It was the oldest Sourdough boy who wrote the letter, blackmailing his own father to line his pockets. He found out that Elias had been to see you and he knew we would blame you. Ruby found another letter he was going to send to Dr. Mouldered. Everyone feels terrible, Mr. Zabbidou. You were right: All we had to do was wait a little longer. Are you a doctor, too? Did you know about his heart?"

I could have laughed out loud. Now they thought Joe was a hero again. What was it then that bothered me so much? Jeremiah had so many enemies he was always going to meet a sticky end one way or the other, so did it really matter how? But I couldn't bear the thought that Joe was involved in such a wretched business. All those times I had worried about having sneaked a look in the Black Book. There were far greater sins being committed than that!

"His heart?" repeated Joe. "Yes, I suspected something was amiss with the fellow."

Perigoe's eyes went to the bag on his shoulder. Her eyelid flickered rapidly and she blushed.

"Are you leaving?"

"Indeed I am. I think Pagus Parvus can do without me now."

A tear squeezed out of the corner of her eye, but she wiped it away quickly and sniffed. "Then I am glad I caught

you. I want to give you something." She handed over a small book. "It doesn't matter anymore, now that Jeremiah's gone. Too many bad memories. I mean, who cares about sheep?"

Joe hesitated. "You do realize what this is worth, don't you?"

Perigoe nodded. "I couldn't take the money. You deserve it, after all you've given us."

"If it is your wish, I accept." Joe tucked the book into his cloak, but not before I managed to catch the title. *The Loneliness of the High Mountain Shepherd.*

"And there's this, too. I nearly forgot. Dr. Mouldered found it. I thought it might be important."

She gave him a piece of paper and he kissed her hand. Then she whispered goodbye and hurried away.

"You see," said Joe as he pocketed the folded page, "inheritance. When I sell the book, the money will keep us going for many months."

"Inheritance?" I scoffed. "You mean you get your money from dead people."

Joe smiled. "I suppose that is close enough to the truth."

"People you have killed."

"I have never killed anyone for money, Ludlow. It is not in my nature."

"You'll be telling me next it's against the rules."

Joe sighed and put down his satchel. "All these weeks you have been such a help to me, Ludlow, and I am immensely grateful. You have been honest and loyal and I know it wasn't easy for you. But more than that, I had thought I saw something in you, something I have been seeking for years. That first night when I found you outside in the snow, you reminded me of myself when I was a young man, and I could see a future for you. That is why I want you to come with me. I have such hopes for your talent. I want us to continue to work together. I can show you the world. Tell me, why won't you come?"

Why not, indeed? Of course I wanted to go, desperately. If he had asked a day ago, even hours ago, I would have had no hesitation. But now things were different. I wasn't sure he was the person I had thought him to be. I wasn't even sure who I was anymore.

"You could have a marvelous future, Ludlow. There is so much I could teach you."

"Like murder?" At last I said it, and the relief was indescribable—as was the fear that came with it.

"Ah," he said and his face lit up knowingly. "I wondered when you would come out with it. Presumably you believe I murdered Jeremiah?"

I nodded slowly. "Can you prove to me that you didn't?"

"I..." began Joe, but then another voice hailed us from the shop door. It was Horatio, breathless and sweating from running up the hill.

"I had to come," he said as he crashed through the debris. "I have to tell you, Joe, before you go, I've done something terrible. It wasn't his heart. It was me that did it. I killed him."

Joe took him by the arm and sat him down.

"What is it, Horatio? What do you think you have done?"

"I killed Jeremiah Ratchet. I poisoned his pie and had Polly give it to him. I know I swore I'd never cook up such a dish again but I just had to do something. Dr. Mouldered said you weren't going to help us. I couldn't stand it anymore."

"Listen to me," said Joe, "you mustn't blame yourself. What's done is done. Dr. Mouldered said he had a heart attack and it is best to accept that. Don't say anything about this to anyone, but make sure the remains of the pie are taken away in case someone else eats it. There are plenty who are hungry enough."

"Are you sure, Mr. Zabbidou?" Horatio looked up with red-rimmed eyes.

"Certain. Just get rid of the pie before someone innocent comes to harm."

"I don't know how to thank you, Mr. Zabbidou," said Horatio. "I don't deserve your help."

"The pie," repeated Joe. "Fetch the pie."

As soon as Horatio was gone Joe put his hands on my shoulders and looked me straight in the eye. "So, Ludlow, now do you trust me?"

I was speechless. I had been so certain. "So you didn't do it?" I stammered. I could hardly look at him. "Can you forgive me?" Then a terrible thought struck me. "Do you still want me to come with you?"

Joe laughed. "Ludlow, my dear fellow, of course I do. How could you possibly think otherwise? Come with me now and

I promise if you don't like what you see, and think you cannot live with what you know, then you and I can go our separate ways and our paths need never cross again."

My heart swelled to bursting point with excitement and I grinned so widely I could feel my skin stretching. I wasted no more time. I collected my purse from the fireplace and pulled my cloak tightly around me. But there was still something I had to say.

"I haven't always been honest with you," I began, but Joe shook his head.

"It'll keep," he said. "Now we must go."

We slipped out through the shattered door, carrying no more than we had when we had arrived in the village all those weeks ago. I looked over my shoulder, but the street was empty. A single light shone in Jeremiah's window, but other than that the houses were dark and we left as we came, unseen.

CHAPTER FORTY

FRAGMENT FROM
THE MEMOIRS OF LUDLOW FITCH

We journeyed on foot for two days and two nights. All the time we were climbing and all the time it was snowing. We had no chance to talk. Our efforts were concentrated on plowing through the drifts and fighting against the wind. It was vital that we stayed together. If we had become separated I had no doubt we would have been lost to each other forever. I did not know if we were going north or south, east or west. There was no sun to guide us and no moon at night.

As we traveled I had a chance to think, to mull over the recent past. Although I was elated that Joe had not murdered Jeremiah (and ashamed that I could have accused him of such a thing), I still felt that had Joe not arrived in Pagus Parvus when he did, Jeremiah would probably still be alive. There was also the matter of Joe's "inheritance," as he liked to call it. Joe had said, and I believed him, that he never killed for money. But money and death seemed inextricably linked when he was around.

There were other unanswered questions, of course, and I had come on this trip for those answers, but as the temperature dropped and the snow became thicker, I wondered if I had been so wise. But there was nothing left for me in Pagus Parvus and I soldiered on, trying to stay cheerful. Toward the end of the journey I was so tired I could hardly lift my feet, and Joe carried me on his back, tucked under his cloak, for the last few miles. I could still hear the storm howling, but the steady rhythm of his footfall, even with the limp, sent me into a delicious slumber. I remember very little after that until I woke up again to find that I was stretched out on the ground.

I was lying under my own cloak on a bed of leafy branches on a hard floor. There was no snow, no wind, no chill in the air. I lay for a few minutes unmoving, enjoying the warmth and comfort. I stared up at a ceiling of rock and when I put out my hand I could feel that the floor was sandy. I sat up and looked around cautiously. I was in a low-roofed cave lit by orange-flamed torches jutting out from the walls. The last time I had seen such burning brands, the night Jeremiah died, they had not cast such a comforting light. If I concentrated I could just hear the wind crying outside, but it sounded very far away. There was a fire at my feet, over which hung a blackened kettle. I could smell something familiar bubbling within. Joe was sitting cross-legged on the other side holding out a bowl.

"Soup?"

After we ate it was time to talk. For once Joe seemed happy to answer my questions. He looked different somehow, relaxed, as if he was in a familiar place.

"It is time for the truth," he said. "If we are to continue our journey together, you must trust me. If there is anything you wish to know, now is the time to ask."

Where to begin! I was so nervous I was shaking, but I knew what I wanted to say. I had rehearsed this moment for days. "Tell me your rules."

Joe nodded and began.

"There are only two, both simple, but it is their simplicity that makes them so difficult to follow. I think you know the first."

I did. "You must not change the course of things."

"Exactly. That is not to say I have no influence. The very fact that I arrive in a place affects the future in some way, but wherever I go, each person is responsible for his own actions. Of the two rules, I think this is the harder to obey. I have seen some terrible things, Ludlow, and it makes it so difficult not to interfere. Nigh on every day in Pagus Parvus I was tempted to ignore the rule. The villagers needed my help so badly, but I had to be deaf to their pleas. I don't really know what they wanted me to do—perhaps they wished me to murder Jeremiah"—here he smiled wryly—"but I could only carry on as normal and hope they could wait. To

behave in any other way would have led to disaster. *Dura lex sed lex*. The law is hard but it is the law."

"And the other rule?"

"You are familiar with that one, too. Everyone, no matter who they are, deserves a chance to redeem themselves, to say sorry, to ask for mercy. Even people like Jeremiah Ratchet. You will remember I gave him that opportunity when he came for the book."

I remembered the sight of Jeremiah pleading for help and I shuddered.

"Of course, he didn't really want my help," continued Joe, "but still I had to offer it to him. You were afraid that if he confessed I would use his secret against him. It broke my heart to see your faith in me waver, although I was immensely pleased that you were so concerned for the fate of the villagers. I knew then I hadn't misjudged you. Your loyalty to them is a quality to be admired. We act for the people, Ludlow. Never forget that.

"I will not deny that Jeremiah's own fate was sealed one way or the other when I came to Pagus Parvus, but he killed himself long before I ever turned up: by his selfishness, his avarice, his cruel nature.

"These are the rules, Ludlow, and I live by them regardless."

He looked at me expectantly and I was ready. "The money you used in Pagus Parvus, where did it come from?"

"A dead person, as you suggested, but before you accuse me of foul play let me assure you it was all perfectly legitimate. Before I came to the village I spent some time in a small town near the border. Business was good. In fact, you will find some of their secrets at the beginning of the Black Book. There is an interesting one about a coffin maker . . ."

My heart sank and I flushed bright red and covered my face with my hands. "You knew."

Joe grinned. "Of course I knew. It was written all over your face when I came back."

"Aren't you angry?"

"I was, I suppose, at the time. More with you than with Polly. But at least you started at the beginning."

"We wouldn't have read anymore," I said. "We both felt terrible afterward."

"I'm glad," replied Joe, laughing. "So you should. It would have been easy enough to make you confess, but I thought I should let you live with your guilt. And the book under your cushion—I'm sure to feel that every night was punishment enough. As I said, *Quae nocent docent.*"

The Latin words at the end of the story.

"It means, 'Things that hurt also teach.' "

Now I felt even worse. "So what happened in that small town?" I asked, anxious to know everything.

"After some weeks it came to my attention that the local physician was deliberately poisoning his patients and stealing their money and belongings. After he died the locals rewarded me quite handsomely with a share of his stolen wealth. And then I moved on."

"But how did he die?"

"Not by my hand, I swear it."

"Then how? More poisoned pie?"

Joe laughed. "No, it was an accident, I promise. But let's not dwell on that. There's more important business to attend to. Follow me."

Joe picked up his satchel and crossed the cave to the opposite wall, where I noticed for the first time the entrance to a tunnel. I hesitated at the opening, it was narrow and dark, but Joe had already stepped through, so I took a torch from the wall and ran after him.

CHAPTER FORTY ONE

As we made our way down the rocky tunnel it became narrower and narrower. Joe could no longer stand up straight and I could not walk beside him. Farther down, the air became heavy and thick as if it had not moved for many years. The torch dimmed to an amber glow, and I feared it might go out altogether. I felt and heard living things fly past me, bats perhaps, but I never saw them, just sensed something brushing against my cheeks and catching at my hair.

"Don't worry, Ludlow," called Joe over his shoulder. "You will come to no harm."

Now we were descending. The slope was gentle at first but quickly became steeper, and I had to hold on to the sides of the tunnel to stay upright. The air pressure was increasing all the time and there was a dull ache in my ears. Finally, when I thought I could bear it no longer, the ground leveled off and the tunnel widened again and the roof raised enough for us both to stand erect. Up ahead I could see Joe

framed in an archway, his slim figure silhouetted in the yellow light. As soon as I reached him he put his hands over my eyes and guided me the last few feet. I knew when we stepped out of the tunnel because the atmosphere changed and was immediately fresher and cooler. The air was filled with high-pitched moans and wails, and low booms and rumbles that seemed to come and go. My own heartbeat filled my ears.

"Let me see," I whispered. "Let me see."

When Joe took his hands from my eyes I thought that I must be in a dream, that I had stepped from reality into a world that existed only in the imagination, for how else could this be? We stood like tiny insects in an endless hall with an arched roof that was maybe a hundred feet above us. Huge grooved pillars, thicker than ancient tree trunks, reached up to hold aloft the copper ceiling. Light came from shallow dishes of flaming oil that sat upon slender white marble plinths shot through with silver. The walls were dark, made not of rock but from some other material, the nature of which I couldn't determine; and the floor, surely a masterpiece of craftsmanship in itself, was decorated with tiny pieces of colored stone set into the earth.

I stared and stared. I think my mouth was wide open. As I looked around the magnificent room I felt as if I were seeing for the first time. I couldn't take it all in. My eyes flicked from side to side and with every blink I saw something else. The pillars, at first glance smooth, were actually intricately carved. Tiny vines snaked around and upward, and from between the leaves pairs of eyes peeped out. They were so life-like I almost expected them to blink. The floor, when examined closely, was actually a myriad of pictures, each a self-contained scene of rare beauty. Within these I saw monsters and angels, fairies and small folk, scaled creatures of the sea and the air, some hideous, some alluring, all spectacular.

My gaze was drawn in to the area at my feet, just in front of the entrance to the palatial hall. I stood on the edge of a pale mosaic and depicted within were three figures: One sat at a spinning wheel, a second held a measuring rod to the thread, and the third stood over her with a pair of gleaming shears. Their faces were haggard and they seemed to be in dispute.

"Who are these hags?" I asked, for they were truly ugly, and my words echoed around the walls. "Whoooo..."

"The three sister Fates," said Joe. "One spins the thread of life, the other measures it, and the third cuts it off with her shears. They argue constantly as to which sister is the most important of the three."

"The one with the shears?" I ventured.

Joe smiled. "Certainly she is considered the most menacing, but there is no answer, for without one the other two could not exist."

"The three Fates," I murmured. "Why should they be here?"

I stepped a little farther into the hall and realized with a shock that the black walls were not walls at all but the

unmarked spines of books crammed together on shelves that rose to the ceiling.

"Take one," said Joe.

So I ran over and pulled one, with difficulty, so tightly was it held by its neighbors, from the shelf. As soon as I had it in my hands I knew what it was. There were those same golden words on the cover:

Verba Volant Scripta Manent

"Oh, Lord," I gasped in complete amazement. "Is this a book of secrets?"

Joe nodded. I opened it carefully, for it was ancient and the leaves were crumbling into dust. I struggled to read the unfamiliar handwriting. Every page was filled top to bottom, each recording the precious stories of long-dead strangers. I closed it and stood back from the shelves. Joe was watching me closely. Could it be possible...?

"Are they all books of secrets?"

"Yes. Every one. From every corner of the globe."

There must have been thousands. And within each book maybe fifty, a hundred secrets or more. I couldn't begin to understand what this meant. It was a few moments before I could speak again. "Who put them here?"

"I did," said Joe. "And others, of course. You are looking at centuries of confessions, Ludlow. My life's work and that of every other Secret Pawnbroker who ever existed."

"But I thought... you mean you're not the only one?"

Joe smiled. "I hope you are not disappointed," he said, "but there have been many of us, and there will be many more. For now the honor goes to me. But I cannot go on forever. Whatever you may think of me, I am still human. I, too, will return to dust one day."

Suddenly I grew nervous. My voice shook, my knees trembled, but I had to ask. "This is where you came, isn't it? When you went away."

Joe nodded. "It is something I have to do. I am responsible in part for this place. In a way this hall is my only home."

"So why have you brought me here?"

"Because it could be your home, too. Soon you will have to make a choice and then, if you do as I think you will do, you need to know all this. Come with me. There is someone I want you to meet."

I followed him, all the time turning my head left and right, up and down, to see more, to take it all in and keep it there. We walked between the pillars to the far end of the hall until we came to a large, dark wood desk with thick, ornately carved legs. It was stacked high with uneven piles of books. As we approached I heard the sound of a chair being pushed back. A man, hidden when seated, stood up and came forward with both arms extended. He wore a long velvet cloak, the color of which changed with every movement he made. His face was concealed beneath a hood, but he pushed it back and I looked into a pair of eyes I had thought never to see again.

"Mr. Jellico?" I managed to gasp just before he gave me a hug so tight I feared it would break my bones.

When he finally released me he patted me on the back and shook my hand over and over. "I'm so pleased to see you again, Ludlow," he said and there was a tear in his eye. "I had no idea what to think. I went away for a few days and when I came back you no longer visited. I thought the worst, of course, that you had met some terrible fate at the hands of your parents, but thank the heavens I was wrong. I could not have forgiven myself if anything had happened to you. You can't know how relieved I am to see it has all worked out in the end. Thanks in part, I'm sure, to my good friend here, Mr. Zabbidou."

I looked from one to the other, completely dumb-founded.

"You do know each other!" I exclaimed. "Joe, why didn't you say?" I couldn't stop shaking my head in disbelief. "But I thought there was only one Secret Pawnbroker."

Mr. Jellico laughed. "I am not a Secret Pawnbroker, nothing so exalted as that. No, I merely look after this place, in a fashion. They call me *Custos*, the Keeper, and this is my realm, *Atrium Arcanorum*, the Hall of Secrets."

"But your shop, in the City?"

"Hmm, yes," he mused, stroking his close-shaven chin. I noticed for once his nails were clean and polished. Even his skin glowed. "It is not easy being in two places at once. I'm sorry I couldn't always be there for you, but as you can see, I have other obligations."

While I reeled from one revelation after another, Joe and Mr. Jellico stepped aside and wandered away down the hall,

deep in conversation. I stood by the desk, dizzy with thinking and seeing. I turned in slow circles and tried to understand. A thousand "What ifs" ran through my head. What if
I had never come to Pagus Parvus? What if I had chosen another carriage other than Jeremiah Ratchet's? What if Ma
and Pa . . .

I made myself stop. I had to. I could have gone on forever.

It was all supposed to happen exactly as it did, I decided.
It wasn't luck, it was meant to be.

Farther down the hall I saw Lembart take the Black Book of
Secrets from Joe—the very book in which I had recorded
the confessions of Pagus Parvus—and push it onto a shelf.
When I looked again I could not tell you where it was. Joe
beckoned me over.

"Well, what do you think?" he asked.

"I think this is the most incredible place I have ever seen,"
I whispered. "It . . . it almost scares me."

"That's what I thought when I first came here," said Mr.
Jellico wistfully, "but that was a very long time ago."

"Lembart does a fine job keeping it in order," said Joe.

"I do my best," he said modestly and moved away, leaving
us alone.

Joe turned to face me and now his expression was somber.
"I have something to give you, Ludlow, if you want it,"
he said.

He reached under his cloak and handed me a black book, leather-bound with a red ribbon to mark the page, as yet blank inside, but on the cover in the bottom right-hand corner I saw the gold letters:

LF

"A Black Book? Of my own?" I was more than a little dazed.

"It's not an easy life," said Joe thoughtfully. "I think you know that, but it has its own rewards. If you do not wish to pursue it, now is the time to say so."

I couldn't speak, I could only stare with my mouth agape and my eyes fixed. What did all this mean?

"You wouldn't start right now, of course," he continued, "but one day in the future, and I will be here to help until then."

At last I managed to whisper, "Are you asking me to be a Secret Pawnbroker?"

"Not just 'a' but 'the' Secret Pawnbroker," he replied. "Have I chosen well, Ludlow? Do you think you can do it?"

Now I was finding it difficult to breathe. My tongue seemed to be stuck to the roof of my mouth. This was the most important moment in my life and my body was letting me down. I mustered all my energy and inhaled deeply and tried to calm the hammering against my ribs. "But . . . but how can I?" I stammered. "I am not ready. What do I know of all this?"

"Enough." He smiled. "As for being ready, well, no one can tell what the three sisters will spin for us, but when the time is right, you'll know."

The three sisters, I thought, and slowly I began to understand why their picture was in the mosaic. This room was not just about secrets, it was about Fate. And Joe, this tall, wild-haired man, was an instrument of Destiny. He was the key to my future. His voice cut into my thoughts.

"As long as you believe you are able," he said, "then there is no reason for it not to happen."

"I believe I am able," I said at last with a little more strength.

Joe patted me on the shoulder. "That is all I wanted to hear," he said. "Now I will ask just one more thing of you."

We walked back to the desk, and I could sense between the two of us an invisible connection that wasn't there before. It gave me confidence and made me hold my head high and my back straight. He sat on one chair and I sat on another. From his satchel he took out the brandy and two glasses. He poured an equal measure into each and handed one to me.

"Drink."

I had to laugh. "Once I thought it might be poisoned," I confessed.

Joe looked at me with great amusement as I sipped from the glass. The burning liquid warmed the back of my throat and made me cough. Joe delved into the bag again and pulled out the ink and the quill. Automatically I reached for them, but he held them back.

"I will write," he said.

I was confused. "But who down here shall tell his secret to us?"

Still holding my book, he opened it on the first page.

"You will, Ludlow," he said. "The first story in your first Black Book will be your own." He looked straight into my eyes and my head filled with singing like angels', and because I thought I might suddenly float away, I wanted to tell him everything.

"It is time for you to give up your secret."

CHAPTER FORTY TWO

EXTRACT FROM
THE BLACK BOOK OF SECRETS

Ludlow's Confession

My name is Ludlow Fitch and I have a shameful confession.
I have carried it with me to Pagus Parvus and now to this
deep underground library of secrets. Though I am fearful
that you will think less of me, I wish to reveal it, for I can
bear it no longer.

You know whence I come, you know what sort of life I led
in the City. I am not proud of my past, but neither will I
deny it. I did what I had to do to survive.

As the drink took hold of Ma and Pa I realized they
would stop at very little in their pursuit of gin. I had never
expected, however, that I should become a mere pawn in
their selfish games. You can imagine my surprise then when
I arrived back one evening to find them lying in wait. As
soon as I stepped foot inside the attic room we called home,
Ma brought down a chair leg on my skull and I crashed to

the floor. I was hardly alive as they dragged me down the stairs feetfirst, my head bouncing off every step, and when Pa flung me over his shoulder my skull throbbed even more. I don't know how long we walked; I lost track of the turns and corners, and I couldn't read the street names on account of my blurred vision. I knew we were still near the Foedus, her smell was strong in my nostrils, and perhaps I have her to thank for the fact that I remained awake as long as I did. Eventually, however, I succumbed to the terrible throbbing in my brain and I lost consciousness. When I opened my eyes, I was in the basement lair of Barton Gumbroot.

I still hate to think of what he tried to do to me. When I managed to escape onto the street I knew that my life was never going to be the same. The three of them chased me all the way to the river. I could see the Bridge up ahead and I thought if I could just get there, maybe I could find help in one of the taverns. But I was slowing, I couldn't see properly, and I was running out of breath. Then, to my utter horror, Pa caught me.

He grabbed me by the shoulder and spun me around. We both fell in the dirty slush and he jumped on me and clasped his hands around my throat. His strength was superhuman. His desire for money, for gin, made it so, but my desire to live was greater. I reached up and burst his arms apart and at the same time I kneed him in the stomach. He fell sideways and rolled on his back and then the tables were turned. I sat upon his chest and held his arms down over his head.

I looked into his cruel face and saw nothing to stop me. I closed my hands around his scrawny neck and squeezed until he was blue in the face and his eyeballs began to bulge. He writhed and kicked and tried to wrest my hands away. He was unable to speak, but his eyes were begging for mercy and I couldn't ignore their plea. Whatever else he might be, he was still my father. With a shout I let go and stood over him as he wheezed and coughed for breath.

"Why did you do it?" I gasped.

"I'm sorry, son," he croaked in a voice full of remorse and, like a fool, I thought he meant it. Ma and Barton were coming, I could hear them. I turned for no longer than a second and Pa was up again and had his arms tight as a noose around my neck. I elbowed him sharply to make him let go and then I shoved him hard as I could and he stumbled backward down the steep bank.

"No," he cried, "noooo," before landing on his back in the dark waters of the Foedus. I watched in disbelief as she sucked him under in a matter of seconds. I could see his white face, his mouth wide open and bubbling, just below the surface, and then he was gone. "Pa," I whispered and for a second I was rigid with shock. Then I came to my senses and stumbled onto the Bridge, where I saw Jeremiah's carriage just pulling away. With a supreme effort I managed to climb onto the back. As we gathered speed I could still see Ma. She was crying and screaming and Barton was shaking his fist at me and cursing.

I murdered my own father, Joe. Whatever he had done to

me, surely he didn't deserve that. I could have saved him. I could have gone down and dragged him out. I cannot forgive myself. I have dreamed of it every night and always I see his face looking up at me from the water. ✳

Joe put down his quill, laid a sheet of blotting paper between the pages, and closed the book. Tears streamed down Ludlow's cheeks.

"I'm just a filthy murderer," he sobbed. "Why would you want me with you?"

"Ludlow," said Joe softly, "it was never your intention to kill your father. If you were going to, you would have strangled him when you had the chance; instead you pitied him. You don't even know for sure that he's dead."

"I pushed him into the Foedus. No one gets out of that poisonous river alive."

"Maybe your ma and Barton pulled him out. Unless you go back, you'll never know. As for coming with me—I knew what you did. I've always known."

"You knew?" sniffed Ludlow. "How?"

"I don't think you've had a full night's sleep since you came to Pagus Parvus. I have heard you wandering around, I have seen you standing at the window, and I have listened to your nightmares. It wasn't difficult to work out what had happened. Believe me, your story is not the worst to go in a Black Book. But for now it doesn't matter. Let's concentrate on what's ahead, not what has gone before."

Ludlow sat quietly for a moment, and then he asked, "Do you have a secret, Joe?"

He smiled. "I do and it is in the very first Black Book I owned."

"And where is that book?"

"Hmm," he mused. "You'd have to ask Mr. Jellico about that. Though it is so long ago I doubt even he would know which shelf it is on!"

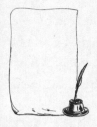

CHAPTER FORTY-THREE

FRAGMENT FROM
THE MEMOIRS OF LUDLOW FITCH

Saluki was croaking loudly in her tank when we emerged, quite breathless, into the upper cave. Joe took her out and stroked her.

"Would you like to hold her?"

"Of course, but will she allow it?"

"Let's find out."

So I held out my quivering hand and Joe placed her gently on my palm. She was as light as a feather. I had never noticed before how delicate she was. Her back was mottled bright red and yellow and her long slender legs were the green of young shoots in the spring, while her underbelly was white with pale blue patches.

"She trusts you," he said simply. I laughed. I had never thought to hold such a beautiful creature in my life. He took her back and carefully placed her in the drawstring bag, and as he did so a piece of paper, the one Perigoe had

given him in the shop, fluttered from under his cloak and landed on the floor.

"What's this?" I asked.

"Read it," he said, and there was a strange look in his eye. I held it up to the dim light and if I had thought I could be surprised no more, then I was to be proved wrong. What I saw and read finally gave me the answer to the ultimate question.

"You clever devil," I said. "So that's how you did it. It wasn't Horatio's pie at all."

"I did it?" he queried and he looked at me with mild irritation. "Are you sure?"

"No, you're right," I exclaimed as I realized what he meant. "You didn't. It's like you said—Jeremiah brought it on himself." And then I realized something else, something far more terrible. "Oh, my Lord," I whispered. "Oh, my Lord."

"What is it, Ludlow?"

"How did you know Saluki trusted me?" I asked slowly.

Joe shrugged. "*Fortuna favet fortibus.*"

Fortune favors the brave.

My hands were shaking as I gave him back the paper. "Please don't take any more chances," I said. "At least not with me."

"Ah, Ludlow," he said, grinning, "I'm disappointed in you. What is life if not a gamble?"

CHAPTER FORTY-FOUR

Page torn from

Amphibians of the Southern Hemisphere

(Returned to Joe by Perigoe and then given to Ludlow in the cave)

Phyllobates tricolor

This colorful tree frog is a member of the Poison Dart Frog family (Dendrobatidae) and a native of the rain forests of South America. When the creature is under stress, from a predator, for example, it secretes a powerful poison through special pores on its back. This poison causes the skin to burn and blister and seeps into the bloodstream, bringing about rapid muscle and respiratory paralysis and leading inevitably to death. The native Indians of the area tip their arrows with the poison, hence the name Poison Dart. There is no known cure.

If you see one of these frogs, unless you two are well acquainted, it is advisable not to touch it.

CHAPTER FORTY-FIVE

FRAGMENT FROM
THE MEMOIRS OF LUDLOW FITCH

Outside it was impossible to see where we had emerged, even though we stood no more than a few feet away from the entrance. I shielded my eyes from the glare of the snow and looked at Joe. "Where to now?"

"I think we shall go to the City," he said. "There are many there who might benefit from our services."

"Do we have to?" I had no desire as yet to return to that despicable place.

"We are masters of our own destiny, Ludlow," said Joe. "We can go wherever we choose."

"Then let us leave the City for another day."

"Well, as you wish. Though you cannot avoid it forever." Joe turned in the other direction and began to walk.

"Wait," I said. "Just answer me one more question."

"Of course."

"What is so important about the wooden leg?"

"It'll come in useful one day, Ludlow."

"Is it something to do with your limp?"

"That's two questions."

"Please," I begged, but to no avail. Joe looked at me with the hint of a smile and a twinkle in his eye.

"A man must be allowed at least one secret, Ludlow, don't you think?"

CHAPTER FORTY-SIX

Loose Ends

Horatio Cleaver never did tell anyone about the poisoned pie. In fact, when he went back to collect it he was both surprised and relieved to see that it had not been touched apart from a piece of crust that had been broken off and, by the looks of it, spat out onto the plate. He concluded then with a clear conscience that Dr. Mouldered's diagnosis had been right.

As for Jeremiah, he was buried in Pagus Parvus cemetery in a grave that was a full nine feet deep. Obadiah had dug with an enthusiasm that was hard to contain. You might have thought that the funeral would have been sparsely attended, but the opposite was true. It seemed that everyone for miles around came to see Ratchet's interment. And, of course, there was little weeping. Indeed, there was a general air of hilarity and jollity, and at the gathering afterward drink flowed freely and laughter rocked the walls of the Pickled Trout.

Jeremiah's grave was robbed only a matter of days after he was buried. The culprits were a little disconcerted by those extra three feet but dug them nonetheless. Upon payment to each of twenty shillings and sixpence Jeremiah ended up on a cold slab in an anatomy school in the City. When the inquisitive surgeon cut into his chest he found a most odd thing: Jeremiah's heart was so small it could fit into a jam pot.

After hearing of its size many eminent physicians and surgeons were curious as to how such a small organ could support the life of such a huge man. Some even wondered whether the ancients had been right all along to attribute the source of life to the liver. It is thought that Jeremiah's heart set back medical progress by at least a decade.

Jeremiah had no family and no will, so it was decided that Ratchet's tenants could claim ownership of their properties. Whether this was lawful or not was hardly a consideration. Sometimes there are advantages to being isolated from the outside world.

As for Polly, with Jeremiah dead and Joe and Ludlow gone, there was little left for her in Pagus Parvus. So a few days later she hitched a ride on Perigoe's trap and took off to the City, still believing it couldn't possibly be as bad as Ludlow made out.

A Note from F. E. Higgins

So there you have it, the tale of Joe Zabbidou and Ludlow Fitch. And let us not forget Saluki, without which frog Destiny could not be fulfilled.

Of course, this is not the end of the story. Where did Ludlow and Joe go? What small village or town or city was next to play host to the Secret Pawnbroker and his apprentice? These questions turned over and over in my head and I knew I had to find the answers. To this end I traveled to a country deep in the heart of the northern mountains until I reached the ancient village of Pachspass. I wonder, does that name excite you as much as it did me when I first came across it? If you say it carefully, it sounds very much like a place we have come to know well.

I rented a tiny attic room in a tall house with small leaded windows that overlook a steep high street. Each night I stand at the window and imagine that I can hear footsteps outside and that I can see a light at the top of the hill. A month has

passed and I am still here, snowbound. Its bright beauty is dazzling but also frustrating, for it prevents the remainder of my journey. As soon as I am able I will be on my way again, unraveling the mystery, and I will take only one thing: the wooden leg. It has not yet yielded its secret to me, but I know that I am closer to finding it now than ever before.

So wish me luck on my journey. I promise whatever I find I will bring it to you as quickly as I can. Until then, as Joe would have said, *Vincit qui patitur*.

F. E. HIGGINS
Pachspass

Addenda

ON THE BUSINESS OF BODYSNATCHING

Obadiah Strang was not alone in the grisly business of bodysnatching. In his day it was a common problem, to the extent that sometimes guards were paid to watch over the newly buried to ensure they remained underground. The human body was a source of great mystery to people. Although ordinary folk were too busy trying to survive to worry about its secretive workings, there were others, scientists and doctors, who were intrigued by the riddle of bone and flesh, and they knew the only way to find out more was to probe deeper.

There was only so much probing you could do with a live body. For a more thorough investigation you needed a dead one. There were laws: Only the bodies of executed criminals could be used in this sort of research, but it would seem that these were not in sufficient supply to meet demand. Thus emerged the business of bodysnatching. At one time it was possible to make a good living selling wickedly procured

corpses to doctors and surgeons, who would dissect them alone or under the curious gaze of anatomy students.

Jeremiah was shocked when his bodysnatching henchmen suggested that Ludlow would provide a fresh corpse, but they would not have been the only ones to think in such a way. Some years later two fellows, William Burke and William Hare, became infamous for just such a thing. They saw in bodysnatching a marvelous business opportunity, but not for them the hard labor of digging up a corpse. The wily pair decided to bypass the grave altogether and to murder people instead. Their first victim was a lodger in Hare's guesthouse. A case of bed but no breakfast, I suppose.

ON THE BUSINESS OF PIE MAKING

When the Sourdough brothers suggested that Horatio Cleaver put "man meat" in his pies they were joking, but it puts me in mind of another man who was deadly serious about his pies: Sweeney Todd, the infamous cutthroat of Fleet Street.

Sweeney lived in London some years after Horatio was butchering in Pagus Parvus. Abandoned by his parents at an early age, Sweeney was apprenticed to a Mr. John Crook, a cutler by trade who fashioned, among other things, razors. It is highly probable that Crook forced Sweeney to steal for him, not an uncommon arrangement between master and apprentice, so it is not surprising that Sweeney eventually ended up in Newgate Prison. Sweeney had developed a keen

instinct for survival by then and managed to persuade the prison barber, who shaved the prisoners in preparation for execution, to take him on as a soap boy, a perk of which job was the opportunity to pick pockets. When Sweeney emerged from prison he was well equipped with the skills to indulge in the evil inclinations that were to earn him a place in history.

He set up a barbershop in Fleet Street, an insalubrious place in those days, and yielded wholly to his thieving and murderous desires. When you sat in Sweeney's barber chair, by all accounts you sealed your own fate. Its design was such that at the touch of a lever the chair would drop into the basement below, to be replaced by an empty chair that came up. Whether Sweeney slit the throat of his customer and robbed him while he was in the chair, or carried out his crimes after the victim had dropped into the basement, is unclear. What *is* certain is that if you went into his shop there was no guarantee you would come out.

The problem with murder is that inevitably there is a body that requires disposal. As luck would have it, Sweeney's shop was built on the site of an old church complete with underground tunnels and catacombs. One of these tunnels led farther down the street to the basement of his accomplice, a certain Mrs. Lovett. Mrs. Lovett also had a shop on Fleet Street.

A pie shop.

It would appear that she and Sweeney came to a gruesome arrangement that suited them both rather well. Sweeney

solved that problem of the bodies; and as for Mrs. Lovett, well, suffice it to say it was reported at the time that her pies were much sought after on account of their quality and taste.

Perhaps if Sweeney had lived in Pagus Parvus he, too, would have been knocking at Joe's door. Certainly his confession would have put Horatio Cleaver's into the shade.

ON THE BUSINESS OF LIVE BURIAL

You may remember that in the coffin maker's confession, Septimus Stern recalled a case where a young man had been buried alive and discovered too late by his family. One wonders how often this did happen in Ludlow's day—after all, the doctors at the time lacked the medical knowledge or expertise that we have today to determine whether a person really is dead. A certain Count Karnice-Karnicki, alive and kicking in the 1800s, had such little faith in the medical profession that he designed a device to prevent his ever being buried alive. In a similar fashion to the coffin maker, he attached a tube to a coffin and ran it to the surface. If there was any movement after burial, breathing perhaps, the rising and falling of the chest, a flag would be activated above ground and a warning bell would ring. By no means was the count alone in his fear. Around the same time a Mr. Martin Sheets designed his own tomb to include a telephone so he could summon help were he to wake up buried but not yet dead.

ON THE BUSINESS OF TOOTH PULLING

Finally, we cannot finish without mention of Barton Gumbroot, the notorious tooth surgeon of Old Goat's Alley. Tooth rot was a serious problem in Ludlow's day and dentistry was a less sophisticated and more brutal affair than it is now. False teeth were available in a wide range of materials, including hippopotamus and walrus teeth, elephant ivory, and, of course, human teeth. There was also the option of a tooth transplant (as Ludlow found out). It had been discovered that when transplanting a tooth, the fresher the donor tooth the better chance it had of taking root in the receiving gum. Widespread poverty meant there were those willing to surrender teeth for money but, unfortunately for Ludlow, Barton Gumbroot didn't always wait for willing volunteers. Jeremiah had thought to sell corpses' teeth at one stage but, unsurprisingly, such teeth failed to take.

GOFISH

F. E. HIGGINS

What did you want to be when you grew up?
I wanted to be a teacher, and did in fact teach for some years, before giving up to write full time.

When did you realize you wanted to be a writer?
When I was quite young, but I allowed life and work to get in the way.

What's your first childhood memory?
Going to a park with my grandmother and seeing peacocks.

As a young person, who did you look up to most?
Probably ABBA!!

What was your worst subject in school?
Geography.

What was your best subject in school?
Foreign languages, especially Latin, but more from a grammatical point of view rather than accents and the interpretation of literature.

What was your first job?
Testing cattle for TB in Ireland.

How did you celebrate publishing your first book?
I bought a new washing machine.

Where do you write your books?
In a small study under the stairs in my house.

Where do you find inspiration for your writing?
Everywhere, but the trick is to make sure you write down ideas when they come to you; otherwise they will be lost, especially your dreams.

Which of your characters is most like you?
I'm not sure my characters are like me; I think it is more that I want to be like them.

When you finish a book, who reads it first?
My editor. It's very difficult to listen to criticism from anyone to whom you are related.

Are you a morning person or a night owl?
Definitely morning. I like to switch off by the end of the afternoon and read and watch TV—technically, of course, this is research!

What's your idea of the best meal ever?
Anything with chocolate and cream and butter and sparkling wine.

Which do you like better: cats or dogs?
Neither. I am not particularly interested in animals.

What do you value most in your friends?
Sense of humor.

Where do you go for peace and quiet?
I work from home and have plenty of peace and quiet during the day.

What makes you laugh out loud?
The Diary of a Nobody by George and Weedon Grossmith.

What's your favorite song?
"Highwayman" by Johnny Cash.

Who is your favorite fictional character?
If I am allowed my own, then Beag Hickory, the potato-throwing dwarf in *The Bone Magician*. I dedicated *The Eyeball Collector* to him.

What are you most afraid of?
Sleep paralysis.

What time of year do you like best?
Winter.

What's your favorite TV show?
Mad Men and old episodes of *Columbo*.

If you were stranded on a desert island, who would you want for company?
Someone who spoke a foreign language I didn't know at all, and then we could see how long it took to understand each other. Or someone who could teach me boogie-woogie piano.

If you could travel in time, where would you go?
Into the past, possibly medieval England, or ancient Rome.

What's the best advice you have ever received about writing?
Elmore Leonard said, "Try to leave out the parts that people skip."

What do you want readers to remember about your books?
What goes around comes around, the idea of natural justice.

What would you do if you ever stopped writing?
I would be an actor or a singer in a band (this is highly unlikely). Or I might run a small sandwich shop.

What is your worst habit?
Procrastination.

What do you consider to be your greatest accomplishment?
Finishing a book!!

Where in the world do you feel most at home?
At home. I like to travel but I always look forward to coming home.

What do you wish you could do better?
Play the piano.

What would your readers be most surprised to learn about you?
How incredibly lazy I am. It's a miracle that I achieve anything at all.

A killer is on the loose.

Bodies are being raised from the dead.

How did Pin Carpue end up in the middle of it all?

More of the marvelously creepy world of
F. E. Higgins is revealed in

The Bone Magician

CHAPTER ONE

Strange Company

A corpse on the cusp of putrefaction could hardly be considered the most entertaining company on a winter's evening, but Pin Carpue didn't do what he did for the conversation. He did it for the money. Tonight, however, things were different. If the body he was watching—her name, when alive, was Sybil—had revived and tried to engage him in some sort of discourse, he couldn't have replied even if he had wanted to.

For Pin had just succumbed to a soporific drug.

Hardly able to move, certainly unable to speak, he lay in a semi-comatose haze on a bench in the corner of the dark room. The last thing his soggy brain recalled was leaving his lodgings. As for his immediate whereabouts, it was a mystery.

With a supreme effort Pin finally managed to open his heavy eyes. He stared into the gloom, but it was difficult to make any sense of his surroundings when he had double vision. His thoughts were like clouds floating in the sky, shapeless and gently moving. Overall, he decided, this feeling, this woozy buzzing between his ears, was not wholly unpleasant.

Somewhere in the room soft voices were whispering and, if Pin had allowed them, they would have lulled him back to sleep. But another part of him was conscious enough to know that he wanted to stay awake. For any other boy it most certainly would have been beyond his capabilities to keep his eyes open under such difficult circumstances, but Pin was used to staying awake until the early hours. It was part of the job.

The job of watching corpses.

He also had a powerful ally in his pocket, a glass phial, full to the brim with the waters of the River Foedus. It was a distasteful job, gathering her noxious liquid, but now he was silently thankful that he had filled it earlier. If he could only reach it! His fingers, usually nimble, were like soft rubber and he fumbled just trying to lift the flap of his coat pocket. Eventually he managed to grasp the phial and bring it out. He rested before he engaged in the next struggle, removing the stopper. His hand couldn't do it, so, with a tremendous effort, he raised the bottle to his mouth, though his arm felt as if it was moving through deep water, and pulled the cork out with his teeth. He took a long, deep sniff and immediately his eyes began to smart and the inside of his nose stung sharply as if he had bitten down on a mustard seed.

"Fiends," he exclaimed in his head and blinked. But the brew had the desired effect and a second sniff brought him slowly back to his senses. Thus slightly revived, though quite exhausted, Pin focused his mind on his situation.

Now he remembered where he was. This was the *Cella Moribundi*, the waiting room for the dead, in Mr. Gaufridus's basement. For some reason he had been drugged by those people, the three shadows that were moving around at the table in the center of the room. He did not think to try to escape, his deadened limbs would not have allowed it. Besides, he had a feeling that *they* were not interested in him but in the body lying on the table.

"He's waking up."

The girl's voice sent a shot of panic through Pin's veins. He could see a figure moving slowly toward him out of the darkness. Inside he was gripped with fear and tried to cry out, but he was unable. So he closed his eyes tightly. If she thought he was asleep she might leave him alone. He knew when she was right beside him. She smelt of juniper and the sleeping drug, aromas he would not easily forget. Pin felt her sweet breath on his face.

"Give him some more," instructed a man's voice.

"No, I think he is still under," she said finally. Then all was quiet.

Slowly, cautiously, Pin dared to open his eyes again. The waters of the Foedus and the lingering effect of the girl's drug were a potent combination, leaving him in a sort of in-between world. He noticed that the candles had been relit and, from the voices, he knew there was the old man, the girl, and a younger man (he sounded like a southerner). In his present state there was little he could do. So he lay back to watch, wholly entranced, the strange drama that was about to play out in front of him.

CHAPTER TWO

Grave Matters

Only a few hours earlier Pin had been in complete possession of his senses. He left his lodgings in Old Goat's Alley after a small supper of ale, bread, and a piece of fish on the turn and trudged off through a shower of hail that was rapidly turning to snow. Pin was always glad to see the back of the place. Old Goat's Alley was considered the worst street south of the River Foedus which, if you knew what the rest of the streets were like, was a frightening thought. Whereas other streets might have a redeeming feature or two, perhaps a slight slope to allow the ever-present sludgy waters to flow away, or a more even distribution of potholes, there was nothing that could be said in favor of Old Goat's Alley.

The tall, narrow houses were poorly constructed, hurriedly built, and squeezed into any space available. The rooms had been divided and subdivided so many times that each house was labyrinthine within. This made it very difficult for the constables when chasing criminals. As did the numerous exits and narrow alleys behind the houses. The buildings leaned slightly forward, which gave cause for alarm if you looked up. It also meant that large amounts of snow slid off periodically into the street below. Few people did look up, however, weighed down as they were with their cares (and ever mindful of the pickpockets). Old Goat's Alley was badly lit, which made it a haven for every sort of criminal that existed. Some nights the lamplighter wouldn't turn up at all and although this was inconvenient for a few, it must be said that many inhabitants were happy to carry out their business in the dark.

As for the rest of the City, certainly on the south side of the river, most pavements were in a state of disrepair and the streets themselves were little more than a mire of noxious debris, churned up daily by the horses and carts that wheeled through and the herds of cattle, pigs, and sheep that were driven along on market day. Each evening the mire froze on account of the extreme temperatures that were currently being experienced. It was a winter like no other.

Barton Gumbroot's lodging house was toward the end of the alley. It was a filthy hovel which Barton had split into as many rooms as possible to maximize rental income. Pin was always uneasy about returning to his room, day or night. His fellow residents were without exception a strange lot and each had particularly nasty features or habits, often both. As for Barton Gumbroot, Pin wouldn't trust the man as far as he could throw him. It was well known that he practiced as a tooth surgeon, another lucrative profession, down in the cellar. Night and day everyone heard the shrieks but no one had the stomach to investigate. In fact, Barton had intimated on more than one occasion that he would take a tooth or two in exchange for a week's rent, but Pin had refused. All this and more was going around in Pin's head as he hurried along beside the river. Just before the Bridge he stopped at the top of a set of stone steps that led down to the water.

The rich really are different, he thought ruefully as he looked across the water. The Foedus was always a foul-smelling river, but the odor was hardly noticeable on the north side because of the prevailing wind. Thus even the air the rich breathed was better. From his vantage point Pin could make out the silhouettes of their fine houses. He didn't need daylight to know what they looked like: double-fronted with sparkling glass, fancy woodwork and glossy doors, polished brasswork and red tiles and frowning gargoyles.

And he knew what sort lived in them, the sort who spent their money on frivolous things, for idle amusement to alleviate their boredom. And this money was not worked for. God forbid that those perfumed men over the water with their frilled cuffs and silken breeches might have to do a day's honest toil. And as for their good ladies, with their noses in the air and their skirts so wide they couldn't fit though a door, well, by all accounts, daily they took their ease, drinking tea, drawing, and singing. No, their wealth in the main was inherited but that was no guarantee it was come upon honestly. Money wasn't the only thing the rich inherited. The duplicity of generations was in their blood. Perhaps they didn't commit the same crimes as took place nightly over the river—the rich liked to keep their hands clean—but they still stole from their fellow man and murdered, just in a more sophisticated way and usually with a polite smile on their faces.

It might be a fine thing to live over the river, thought Pin, *but I wonder, is it better to be in a beautiful house looking at an ugly one, or to be in an ugly house looking at a beautiful one?*

Yes, he thought, as he descended carefully to the sticky black mud below, life on this side was harsh and dirty and noisy, but for all its unpleasantness, there was an honesty of sorts among the southerners. You knew what they were from looking at them. They couldn't hide it beneath fine clothes and words.

The tide was out but on the turn. Pin made his way as quickly as he could to the water's edge. It was not unusual to find sailors' trinkets in the mud, fallen from the ships, but tonight Pin was in a hurry and wasn't looking. He took from his pocket a small two-handled glass phial and removed the cork. Holding one handle delicately between thumb and forefinger, he dipped it just under the surface and dragged it along until it was full of the dark water. Then he corked it carefully and ran back to the steps.

The smell of the Foedus was renowned far and wide but,

exposed to something on a daily basis, a person can get used to most things. It was a rare day in Urbs Umida that the stench was so bad people actually remarked upon it. There is a theory that over time native Urbs Umidians developed a sort of immunity to the smell. This theory might also account for their apparent ability to eat rotting food with impunity. If you can't smell it, you can't taste it. For Pin, however, this was not the case. He had a sensitive nose and was acutely aware of the most subtle changes in the river's odor.

By the time Pin reached the churchyard it was snowing heavily. He passed through the gates, head down, narrowly avoiding a young girl who was coming out. She held up her pale hands in fright. Pin caught the faintest scent as he brushed past her, sweeter than one would have expected, and felt moved to mumble an apology before going on through.

As a place of burial St. Mildred's was almost as old as the City itself. Like a bottomless pit, it held far more people below than was indicated by the headstones above. This was not as difficult as it sounded, for the earth was unusually wet and acidic. These factors combined to speed up the process of decomposition considerably. Given that the churchyard was on a hill, all these decaying juices seeped underground down the slope into the Foedus. Just one more ingredient to add to her toxic soup. It was not unknown for bodies to be skeletal within a matter of months—a phenomenon that was often talked about in the Nimble Finger Inn by those in the know.

But Pin wasn't thinking of rotting bodies as he made his way between the uneven rows of headstones. He walked purposefully until he reached a small unmarked wooden cross. It was leaning to the left and he tried to right it with some difficulty, for the earth was frozen solid. A small bouquet of dried white flowers, stiff with the cold, lay at the base of the cross and he picked them up before hunkering down in the snow.

"Well, Mother," he said softly, "I haven't been for a while, and I'm sorry about that, but Mr. Gaufridus is keeping me busy. I'm working again tonight. You know, I'd rather do that than spend a night at Barton Gumbroot's. He's a sly one, always asking about Father. Is he coming back? Did he really do it? I don't know what to say."

Pin paused after each question, almost as if expecting an answer, but none was forthcoming. So he sat there shivering, oblivious to the thickening snowflakes, turning the flowers over and over in his hand.